Korean Tales

Collection of stories translated
from the Korean folklore

Horace Newton Allen

Pharos Books

ISBN: 978-93-55460-23-3
eISBN: 978-93-55460-31-8

©Publisher

Publisher: Pharos Books (P) Ltd.
Plot No.-55, Main Mother Dairy Road
Pandav Nagar, East Delhi-110092
Phone: 011-40395855, +14049995474
WhatsApp: +91 8368220032
E-mail: sales@pharosbooks.in
Website: www.pharosbooks.in
First Edition: 2022

Printed By: Sushma Book Binding House, Okhla
Industrial Area, Phase I, New Delhi-110020

KOREAN TALES
Horace Newton Allen

Contents

PREFACE 5

INTRODUCTION 7

KOREAN TALES

DESCRIPTIVE SEOUL—THE CAPITAL 13

THE RABBIT, AND OTHER LEGENDS STORIES

OF BIRDS AND ANIMALS 21

THE ENCHANTED WINE-JUG OR, WHY

THE CAT AND DOG ARE ENEMIES 29

CHING YUH AND KYAIN OO THE TRIALS

OF TWO HEAVENLY LOVERS 39

HYUNG BO AND NAHL BO; OR, THE

SWALLOW-KING'S REWARDS............................ 59

CHUN YANG THE FAITHFUL DANCING-GIRL WIFE ... 75

SIM CHUNG, THE DUTIFUL DAUGHTER..................... 97

HONG KIL TONG OR, THE ADVENTURES

OF AN ABUSED BOY 109

PREFACE

Repeatedly, since returning to the United States, people have asked me, "Why don't you write a book on Korea?" I have invariably replied that it was not necessary, and referred the inquirers to the large work of Dr. Griffis, entitled "Corea, the Hermit Kingdom," which covers the subject in a charming manner.

My object in writing this book was to correct the erroneous impressions I have found somewhat prevalent—that the Koreans were a semi-savage people. And believing that the object could be accomplished best in displaying the thought, life, and habits of the people as portrayed in their native lore, I have made these translations, which, while they are so chosen as to cover various phases of life, are not to be considered as especially selected.

I also wished to have some means of answering the constant inquiries from all parts of the country concerning Korean life and characteristics.

People in Washington have asked me if Korea was an island in the Mediterranean; others have asked if Korea could be reached by rail from Europe; others have supposed that Korea was somewhere in the South Seas, with a climate that enabled the natives to dispense with clothing. I have therefore included two chapters, introductory and descriptive in character, concerning the subjects of the majority of such questions.

"Globe trotters," in passing from Japan to North China, usually go by way of the Korean ports, now that a line of excellent

Japanese steamships covers that route. These travellers see the somewhat barren coasts of Korea—left so, that outsiders might not be tempted to come to the then hermit country; perhaps they land at Chemulpoo (the port of the capital, thirty miles distant), and stroll through the rows of miserable, temporary huts, occupied by the stevedores, the pack-coolies, chair-bearers, and other transient scum, and then write a long article descriptive of Korea. As well might they describe America as seen among the slab shanties of one of the newest western railroad towns, for when the treaties were formed in 1882 not a house stood where Chemulpoo now stands, with its several thousand regular inhabitants and as many more transients.

H. N. ALLEN.

WASHINGTON, D. C., *July 1, 1889.*

INTRODUCTION

Korea, Corea, or Chosen (morning calm) occupies the peninsula hanging down from Manchooria and Russian Siberia between China and Japan, and extending from the 33d to the 43d parallels of north latitude.

The area, including the outlying islands, is about one hundred thousand square miles. The population, according to the most reliable estimate, is a little more than sixteen millions. Yet, as the people live in cities, towns, and hamlets, the country does not seem to be thickly settled.

The climate varies much at the extremities of the peninsula, owing to the fact that the southern portion is somewhat affected by the warm southern currents that give Japan its tropical climate, but which are warded off from Korea proper by the Japanese islands. The climate of the central and northern provinces is much the same as that of the northern central United States, with fewer changes. The large river at the capital is not uncommonly frozen over for weeks at a time during the winter, so that heavy carts pass over on the ice. Ice is always preserved for general use in summer.

The country is decidedly mountainous, and well watered. Heavy timber abounds in the northeast. The valleys are very fertile and are well tilled, as the people are mainly devoted to agriculture.

The mineral resources have only been developed in a crude way, yet sufficiently to demonstrate the great wealth of the ore deposits. Especially is this true in reference to the gold mines.

The most pessimistic visitors to Korea are unstinted in their praise of the beautiful scenery, which is fully appreciated by the natives as well. From ancient times they have had guide-books setting forth the natural charms of particular localities; and excursions to distant places for the sole purpose of enjoying the views are a common occurrence.

The King rules as absolute monarch. He is assisted by the Prime-Minister and his two associates—the ministers of the Left and Right. Next to these come the heads of the six departments of Etiquette and Ceremonies, Finance, War, Public Works, Justice, and Registration, with the heads of the two new departments that have been added as the result of the opening up of foreign intercourse—the Foreign (or outside) Office, and the Home (or interior) Office. This body of officials forms the grand council of the King.

Each of the eight provinces is ruled by a governor, who has under him prefects, local magistrates, supervisors of hamlets, and petty officials, so that the whole scale makes a very complete system and affords no lack of officials.

There are several special officers appointed by the King, one of whom is the government inspector, whose duty it is to go about in disguise, learn the condition of the people, and ascertain if any magistrate abuses his office and oppresses the people unjustly. Any such he may bring to speedy justice.

The present Dynasty has existed 498 years. Being founded by a revolting general named Ye, it is known as the Ye Dynasty. The King's name, however, is never used. He is almost sacred to his people. Those officials of sufficiently high rank to go in before him bow to the ground in his presence, and only speak when spoken to; then they use a highly honorific language only understood at court.

The revenues are paid in kind, hence the annual income of an official may consist of a certain quantity of rice, and other products, in addition to his money compensation. The King, also, has the whole revenue resulting from the sale of the ginseng, for which the country is noted. This forms his private purse.

The currency is the common copper cash, worth some twelve hundred to the Mexican dollar; though now that the new mint is in operation, copper, silver, and gold coins are being made. The old perforated cash will, however, be hard to supplant, owing to its convenience in small transactions.

Banks proper do not exist; though the government does a kind of banking business in granting orders on various provincial offices, so that a travelling official need not be burdened with much ready money. A number of large brokers at the capital assist in the government financial transactions.

All unoccupied land belongs to the King, but any man may take up a homestead, and, after tilling it and paying taxes on it for a period of three years, it becomes his own, and must be purchased should the government need it.

Deeds are given in the form of receipts and quit-claims by the seller. These may be registered with the local magistrate. Wills, as understood in western countries, are not executed; though a father wishing to provide especially for the children of his concubines may make a will, or statement, the proper execution of which devolves upon the eldest son.

Records of the births of males are kept, as are also records of deaths, but these are not always reliable. All males of fifteen years of age are registered at the Hang Sung Poo, or Department of Registration, which issues to them tablets bearing their name and address. Children are also generally provided with these tablets, to prevent their getting lost.

The people are well built and strong, as a rule. They are a loyal, contented race, not grasping, and rather too easy in disposition. They are intelligent and learn with great ease. Possessed of many characteristics in common with their neighbors, the Chinese and Japanese, they yet seem to have a personality indicative of a different parentage, which continually calls forth inquiry as to their origin. In some slight degree they resemble the aborigines of America, and it is believed that their ancestors came from the north:—the question opens up a fertile field for study. Their written records are said to date back three thousand years. Their traditional first king descended from heaven five thousand years ago. With a civilization of such age they might well be excused for so long barring their doors against the new civilization of the young nations of the West. While, as a matter of fact, the difference existing between the two is more one of degree than essence, perhaps more vices may be found in the civilization of the West than are known to this people. And, with a few exceptions, the virtues taught by the modern civilization have been practised for centuries behind the bars of isolation that shut in this self-satisfied people.

The people dress in imported cotton sheetings mostly, padding them well with cotton-wool for winter use, and using the plain bleached white, or dying the cloth a light shade of blue or green. Rice is the staple article of food in the central and southern provinces; wheat enters more largely into the diet of the northern people. Their cattle are as large and fine as may be found anywhere; the people eat much beef, and hides are a prominent article of export. Their houses are well built and comfortable; foreigners adapt them to their own use with little trouble. The houses are heated by means of a system of flues underneath the floor, which is made of large flagstone placed over the flues and well cemented; over all thick, strong, oil paper is placed, making a rich, dark, highly polished floor, through which no smoke can come, though it is always agreeably warm. The houses are all one story, built around a court, and several sets of buildings, each within a separate wall, usually make up a gentleman's compound. The buildings are covered with a thick layer of earth and capped with tile laid on in graceful curves. This roof insures coolness in summer. The rooms are made almost air-tight by the plentiful use of paper on the walls outside and in, as well as for doors and windows.

There are three great classes in Korea: the nobility, the middle class, and the commoners. A commoner, not of the proscribed orders, may rise to nobility by successfully passing the competitive examinations. The officials are appointed from the noble classes.

The language is peculiar to the country, and while written official documents are done in the common character of China and Japan, the spoken language of neither of these people is understood in Korea. The native language of Korea possesses an alphabet and grammar, and is polysyllabic, thus resembling English more than it does Chinese.

In religious matters the Koreans are peculiar in that they may be said to be without a religion, properly speaking. Prior to the advent of the present dynasty, Buddhism reigned, but for 498 years it has been in such disfavor that no priest dare enter a walled city. They still maintain temples in the mountains, but exert but little if any influence. In morals the people are Confucianists, and their reverent devotion to their ancestors may serve in part as a religion. In times of distress they "pray to Heaven," and seem really to be very devoutly inclined.

Christianity came into disfavor through the indiscretion of its early teachers. The distrust is slowly passing away now, and missionaries are openly employed in doing the educational work that must precede any successful attempt to secure the adoption of beliefs so radically different from all existing ideas.

Some of the results of the outside intercourse that has been indulged in for the past eight years may be mentioned. A maritime customs service, under the charge of American and European officers, is in very successful operation. So is a hospital, supported by the government and operated by American physicians, gratuitously furnished by the American Presbyterian Mission. The government supports a school for which American teachers are employed. American military officers have charge of the reorganization of the army and conduct a school for the purpose of instructing the young officers. A mint, machine-shops, powder-mills, silk filatures, an electric light, and a telegraph and cable line are some of the new institutions recently adopted and, as a rule, now in successful operation. Steamships have also been purchased more for the purpose of transporting tribute rice than as a nucleus for a navy. In regard to the relations existing between Korea and China the reader is respectfully referred to a paper delivered before the American Oriental Society by the Chinese scholar, W. W. Rockhill, U. S. Secretary of Legation at Pekin, and contained in Vol. III. of the Society's publications for 1888. In his preface Mr. Rockhill says:

"The nature of Korea's relations with China has for the last thirty years been a puzzle for Western nations. Were they—with the ambiguous utterance of the Chinese Government before them that 'Korea, though a vassal and tributary state of China, was entirely independent so far as her government, religion, and intercourse with foreign States were concerned'—to consider it as an integral part of the Chinese Empire, or should they treat it as a sovereign state, enjoying absolute international rights?

"The problem was practically solved by the conclusion of the treaty between Japan, and later on the United States, and Korea, but this has not materially altered the nature of the relations existing for the last four centuries, at least between China and its so-called vassal. That China has, however, derived profit from the opening of Korea to the commerce of nations, there can be no doubt, for she, too, being at liberty to conclude treaties with Korea and open this new market to her merchants, has done so, like other nations, though she has chosen to call her treaty by the euphonious name of 'commercial and trade regulations for the subjects of China and Korea', and her diplomatic representative in Seoul, 'Minister Resident for political and commercial affairs.' What China's relations with Korea were prior to the opening of the latter kingdom by the treaty of 1883, I propose to show in the following pages, taking as my authorities official Chinese publications and writings of men in official position."

KOREAN TALES

DESCRIPTIVE SEOUL—THE CAPITAL

As "Paris is France," so Seoul may be said to be Korea, for it is the centre from which nearly every thing for the country either originates or is disseminated. Officers ruling over country districts usually have their "house in town," and expect to spend a portion, at least, of their time within the walls of the capital. While some of the provincial capitals are said to contain more people and to be more celebrated for certain reasons, Seoul is the home of the King and the Mecca of his faithful subjects. A description of this city may, therefore, answer for all. The capital is a city of some 300,000 inhabitants, half of whom, perhaps, live in the extensive suburbs without the walls. It lies in a basin of granite sand, surrounded by high mountains and their projecting ridges, over which climbs the high, thick, encircling wall of masonry; pierced at convenient points by massive, pagoda-roofed gates, amply strong enough for defense against the weapons of war in use at the time of building this great relic of seclusion.

The city is traversed by broad avenues from which runs a perfect labyrinth of narrow streets. Originally none of these streets were less than twenty feet wide, and some of the avenues leading up to the imposing gates of the palaces are even now a good two hundred feet in width. But the streets have all been encroached upon by the little temporary thatched booths of the petty retail dealers, so that, with the exception of the approaches to the palaces, the line is broken, the streets made tortuous, and only here and there a broad open spot indicates the original width of the thoroughfare. Originally every street was furnished with its sewer—open in the smaller streets, while the avenues were drained by great covered sewers of stonework. Occasionally the proprietor of one of the little temporary booths would put a foundation under his structure, bridging over the sewer, until now the streets have in many cases become mere crooked alleys, and but for the bountiful rains, the excellent natural drainage, and the character of the soil, the mortality would be very great instead of being less than in ordinary American cities. No attempt is made towards street decoration, as that would attract the attention of thieves. The magnificent grounds of a nobleman, with their artificial lakes, flower gardens, water-worn pillars of ancient rock and quaintly twisted trees, may be enclosed by a row of tumble-down, smoke-begrimed servant-quarters that would never indicate the beauty to be found hidden within its forbidding exterior.

Travellers never seem to realize that a street in the East is apt to be but a "way" between two points, and as the usual Oriental odors greet their nostrils and their eyes rest on the dirty servants and their dirtier hovels, they at once denounce the whole town.

There is attraction enough, however, in a Korean street for any one who is in search of strange sights. Looking down one of the broad thoroughfares of Seoul from a point on the city wall, the sun's rays, falling on the light-colored gowns of the pedestrians as they saunter along amid the bulls and ponies, produce a kaleidoscopic effect that is certainly charming. Passing down into the throng it will be seen to be made up mostly of men, with here and there a group of common women, each closely veiled with a bright green gown, made like the long outer garment of the men, and possessing little sleeves of crimson. This strange garment is never worn, but is always used as a covering for the fair (?) face. Tradition teaches that in ancient times, when wars were frequent, veils were discarded and these gowns were worn by the wives and sisters, that, in case of sudden call to arms, they could be given to their husbands and brothers to be worn to battle—hence the red sleeves, upon which the gory sword was to be wiped.

The peculiar gauze "stove-pipe" hat of the men, about which so much has been said, also has its origin in tradition, as follows: In ancient days conspiracies were common; to prevent these an edict was issued compelling all men to wear great earthenware hats, the size of an umbrella (type of the mourner's hat in Korea to-day, except that the latter is made of finely woven basket-work). This law became very odious, for in addition to the weight of the hats, not more than a very few men could come close enough together to converse, and even then spies could hear their necessarily loud whispering. Little by little, therefore, the law began to be infringed upon till the people got down to the present airy structure of horsehair, silk, and bamboo.

Another story is, that petty wars being too frequent between rival sections, all men were compelled to wear these umbrella hats of clay. In case one became broken the possessor was punished by decapitation—naturally they stopped their fighting and took good care of their hats till the law was repealed.

The custom of wearing white so extensively as they do is also accounted for by tradition. Mourning is a serious business in Korea, for on the death of a father the son must lay aside his gay robes and clothe himself in unbleached cotton of a very coarse texture. He wraps his waist with a rope girdle, and puts on the umbrella hat, which conceals the whole upper portion of his person. For further protection against intrusion he carries a white fan, and, should he smoke, his pipe must be wrapped with white. For three years he must wear this guise and must do no work, so that the resources of even a large and prosperous family may be thus exhausted.

Should a king die, the whole nation would be compelled to don this mourning garb, or rather they would be compelled to dress in white—the mourning color. Once, during a period of ten years, three kings died, necessitating a constant change of dress on the part of the people and a great outlay of money, for a Korean wardrobe is extensive and costly. Tradition has it, therefore, that, to be ready for the caprice of their kings in the future, the people adopted white as the national color.

The nobility and wealthy persons who can afford it, dress in rich gayly colored silks, and even the common people add a little blue or green to their outside robes, so that when they wander about over the beautiful green hills in their favorite pastime of admiring the natural beauties of a remarkably beautiful and well preserved landscape, their bright gowns but add to the general effect. And a long procession of monks emerging from their high mountain temple and descending along the green mountain path might be taken for a company of the spirits with which their literature abounds; especially will this be the case if, as is common, the region of the temple is shrouded with clouds.

But little of home life is seen along the streets, and the favored ones who may pass the great gates and traverse the many courts which lead to the fine inclosures of the nobility would see but little of home life, as the women have quarters by themselves, and are only seen by the men of their own family.

It is pleasant, however, to see the little groups of the working class sitting around the fire which is cooking their evening meal and at the same time heating the platform of paper and cement-covered stones which form the floor of their bed chamber, and on which they will spread their mats and sleep. They will all be found to be smoking, and if tobacco was ever a blessing to any people it is to the lower classes in Korea, who find in it their greatest comfort. No one could see the solid enjoyment taken by a Korean coolie with his pipe without blessing the weed.

As the fires burn low, and one by one the smokers have knocked the ashes from their pipes and sought the warm stone floor, a deep stillness settles over the profoundly dark city. The rich, deep notes of a great centrally located bell ring out as the watchman draws back a huge suspended beam of wood, and releasing it, lets it strike the bronze side of the heavy bell, from which vibration after vibration is sent forth upon the still night-air.

Some weird music, which has been likened to that of Scotch bagpipes, is heard from the direction of the city gates, and the traveller, who is still threading the streets to his abode, feels thankful that he has arrived in time, for now the massive gates are closed, and none may enter without royal permission. The street traveller will also hasten to his home or stopping-place, for between the ringing of the evening chimes and the tolling of the bell to announce the approach of dawn, all men must absent themselves from the streets, which then are taken possession of by the women, who even then, as they flit about from house to house with their little paper lanterns, go veiled lest some passing official should see their faces.[1]

The midnight stillness is broken by the barking of countless dogs, but as cats are in disfavor their serenades are seldom heard. Another sound is often, in busy times heard throughout the whole night. It is peculiar to Korea, and to one who has lived long in the country it means much. It is the drumming of the Korean laundry. To give the light-colored gowns their highly prized lustre they must be well pounded; for this purpose the cloth is wrapped around a long hard roller which is fixed in a low frame, two women then sit facing each other with, in each hand, a round, hard stick, something like a small base-ball bat, and they commence beating the cloth, alternating so as to make quite a musical tinkle.

Heard at some distance this rhythmic rattle is not unpleasant, and one is assured that in the deep night that has settled so like a pall over the city, two persons are wide-awake and industriously

---

1. This law has recently been repealed, owing to the fact that bad men often molested the women, who are usually possessed of costly jewels. The husbands are now allowed on the streets as a protection, since even the police were unable to suppress the outrages alone.

engaged, while, when the tapping ceases for a bit, one is comforted with the thought that the poor things are enjoying a rich bit of gossip, or welcoming a friend who is more fortunate in having finished her ironing in time to enjoy the freedom of the night.

Inside the Palace the night is turned into day as nearly as can be done by the electric light. The business of the government is mostly transacted at night that the wheels of administration may run smoothly during the day. At sun-down several lights may be seen on the summit of the beautiful ever green south mountain which forms the southern limit of the city; as does a grim stony peak on the north serve a similar purpose on that side. The south mountain faces the Palaces. It also commands a good view of the outlying peaks, upon some of which, situated in suitable localities, are stationed watchmen, so placed as to command a view of others farther and farther removed; thus forming lines from the distant borders of the country to the capital. On these peaks small signal-fires are nightly kindled, and as the lights are seen by the watchman on the south mountain, he builds the proper number of fires upon little altars in full view of the Palace. Then a body of gray old officers go in before His Majesty, and bowing their heads to the floor, make known the verdict of the signal-fires, as to whether peace reigns in the borders or not. Soon after this the officials assemble and the business of the government begins, the King giving his personal attention to all matters of importance.

There are three palace inclosures in the city, only one of which is occupied. One is an old ruined place that was built for the use of a ruler who chanced to be regent for his father, and as he could not reside in the Palace proper this smaller place was prepared for him. The buildings now are in ruins, while the large grounds are used by the foreign silk expert as a nursery for mulberry-trees.

The present Palace includes some hundreds of acres, and is the home of more than three thousand attendants. The grounds are beautifully diversified by little lakes of several acres in extent, one of which surrounds a magnificent and stately pavilion, supported on great stone pillars,—a fine picture and description of this, and other parts of the Palace, may be found in Mr. Lowell's "Chosen." The other lake possesses a bright little pagoda-like pavilion, around which plays a steam launch, dividing the lotus flowers which grow in the water, and startling the swan, duck, and other aquatic animals that make this their home.

These lakes are fed and drained by a mountain stream that enters and leaves the Palace inclosure, through water-gates built under the walls. Some of the bridges spanning this brook are quaint pieces of artistic masonry, having animals carved in blocks of stone, represented in the act of plunging into the liquid depths below. This carved stone work abounds throughout the Palace buildings; the largest of which is the great Audience-Hall, with its mast-like pillars supporting a ceiling at an elevation of near one hundred feet above the tiled floor.

The dwelling-houses of the Royal Family are built upon the banks of one of the small lakes, and are surrounded by walls for greater seclusion. The rooms are furnished with costly articles from European markets, together with the finest native furniture. Foreign-trained cooks are employed, and the dinners sometimes given to distinguished foreign guests are in entire accord with modern western methods. Royalty is never present at these banquets, which are presided over by one of the heads of departments; the Royal Family, maybe, witnessing the novel sight from a secluded place where their presence may not be known.

The King only leaves the Palace upon certain occasions, as when he goes to bow before the tombs of his ancestors. On these occasions the streets are cleared of the little straw-thatched booths of the petty retail merchants as well as of all other unsightly objects. The street is roped off and sprinkled with fresh earth, and the people don their holiday garb, for it is indeed a great gala day to them. The procession is a gorgeous relic of mediæval times, with bits of the present strangely incorporated. There may be regiments of soldiers in the ancient fiery coats of mail, preceded or followed by soldiers dressed in the queer hybrid uniforms of the modern army, and bearing the bayoneted rifles of the present day, instead of the quaint matchlock-guns and ugly spears of the ancient guard. The wild, weird music of the native bands may be followed by the tooting of the buglers of the modern soldiery.

The strange one-wheeled chair of an official, with its numbers of pushers and supporters, will probably be followed by an artillery company dragging Gatling guns. His Majesty himself will be borne in a great throne-like chair of red work, supported on the shoulders of thirty-two oddly attired bearers, while high officials in the government service may be mounted on horse back, or borne in less pretentious chairs. The length of the procession varies, but it is seldom less than an hour in passing a given place.

The King is thirty-eight years of age. The Queen is one year his senior. The Crown Prince is fifteen years old, and has no brothers or sisters. Foreigners who have been granted an audience with the King are always pleased with his affability and brightness. He is quick of perception and very progressive. By having foreign newspapers translated to him he keeps fully abreast of the times. He is kind-hearted to a fault, and much concerned for the welfare of his people. His word is law, and an official would never think of failing to carry out his instructions or perish in the attempt. Owing to his great seclusion and the amount of ceremony with which he is hedged in, and the fact that, as a rule, nothing disagreeable must be brought to his notice, he is somewhat at the mercy of his favorites; and a trusted eunuch, having the King's ear continually, may become a great power for good or bad as the case may be. As decapitation is the usual punishment for most crimes, however, and as an official who should deceive the King would probably meet with such an end, the responsibility of the place is apt to sober an otherwise fickle mind and insure honest reports.

THE RABBIT, AND OTHER LEGENDS STORIES OF BIRDS AND ANIMALS

The Koreans are great students of Nature. Nothing seems to escape their attention as they plod through the fields or saunter for pleasure over the green hills. A naturally picturesque landscape is preserved in its freshness by the law that forbids the cutting of timber or fuel in any but prescribed localities. The necessity that compels the peasants to carefully rake together all the dried grass and underbrush for fuel, causes even the rugged mountain sides to present the appearance of a gentleman's well kept park, from which the landscape gardener has been wisely excluded.

Nature's beauty in Korea may be said to be enhanced rather than marred by the presence of man; since the bright tints of the ample costume worn by all lends a quaint charm to the view. The soil-begrimed white garments of the peasants at work in the fields are not especially attractive at short range; but the foot-traveller, clad in a gorgeous gown of light-colored muslin, adds a pleasant touch to the general effect, as he winds about the hills following one of the "short-cut" paths; while the flowing robes of brightly colored silk worn by the frequent parties of gentry who may be met, strolling for recreation, are a positive attraction. Nor are these groups uncommon. The climate during most of the year is so delightful; the gentry are so pre-eminently a people of leisure, and are so fond of sight-seeing, games, and music, that they may be continually met taking a stroll through the country.

As has been said, nothing out-of-doors seems to have escaped their attention. The flowers that carpet the earth from snow till snow have each been named and their seasons are known.

The *mah-hah* in-doors throws out its pretty sessile blossoms upon the leafless stem sometimes before the snows have left, as though summer were borne upon winter's bare arm with no leafy spring to herald her approach. Then the autumn snows and frosts often arrive before the great chrysanthemums have ceased their blooming, while, between the seasons of the two heralds, bloom myriads of pretty plants that should make up a veritable botanical paradise. Summer finds the whole hill-sides covered with the delicate fluffy bloom of the pink azaleas, summoning forth the bands of beauty seekers who have already admired the peach and the plum orchards. Great beds of nodding lilies of the valley usher in the harvest, and even the forest trees occasionally add their weight of blossoms to the general effect.

The coming and going of the birds is looked for, and the peculiarities and music of each are known. As a rule, they are named in accordance with the notes they utter; the pigeon is the *pe-dul-key*; the crow the *kaw-mah-gue*; the swallow the *chap-pie*, and so on. One bird—I think it is the oriole—is associated with a pretty legend to the effect that, once upon a time, one of the numerous ladies at court had a love affair with one of the palace officials—a Mr. Kim. It was discovered, and the poor thing lost her life. Her spirit could not be killed, however, and, unappeased, it entered this bird, in which form she returned to the palace and sang, "*Kim-pul-lah-go,*" "*Kim-pul, Kim-pul-lah-go,*" then, receiving no response, she would mournfully entreat—"*Kim-poh-go-sip-so,*" "*Kim-poh-go-sip-so.*" Now, in the language of Korea, "*Kim-pul-lah-go*" means "call Kim" or "tell Kim to come," and "*Kim poh go sip so*" means "I want to see Kim." So, even to this day, the women and children feel sad when they hear these plaintive notes, and unconsciously their hearts go out in pity for the poor lone lover who is ever searching in vain for her Kim.

Another bird of sadness is the cuckoo, and the women dislike to hear its homesick notes echoing across the valleys.

The *pe chu kuh ruk* is a bird that sings in the wild mountain places and warns people that robbers are near. When it comes to the hamlets and sings, the people know that the rice crop will be a failure, and that they will have to eat millet.

The crow is in great disfavor, as it eats dead dog, and brings the dread fever—*Yim pyung.*

The magpie—that impudent, noisy nuisance,—however, is in great favor, so much so that his great ugly nest is safe from human disturbance, and his presence is quite acceptable, especially in the morning. He seems to be the champion of the swallows that colonize the thick roofs and build their little mud houses underneath the tiles, for when one of the great lazy house-snakes comes out to sun himself after a meal of young swallows, the bereaved parents and friends at once fly off for the saucy magpie, who comes promptly and dashes at the snake's head amid the encouraging jabbering of the swallows. They usually succeed in driving the reptile under the tiles.

Should the magpie come to the house with his (excuse for a) song in the morning, good news may be expected during the day; father will return from a long journey; brother will succeed in his (civil-service) examination and obtain rank, or good news will be brought by post. Should the magpie come in the afternoon with his jargon, a guest—not a friend—may be expected with an appetite equal to that of a family of children; while, if the magpie comes after dark, thieves may be dreaded.

This office of house-guard is also bestowed upon the domestic goose. Aside from its beauty, this bird is greatly esteemed for its daring in promptly sounding an alarm, should any untimely visitor enter the court, as well as for its bravery in boldly pecking at and, in some cases, driving out the intruder.

The wild goose is one of the most highly prized birds in Korea. It always participates in the wedding ceremonies; for no man would think himself properly married had he not been presented by his bride with a wild goose, even though the bird were simply hired for the occasion. The reason for this is that these observing people once noticed that a goose, whose mate was killed, returned to the place year after year to mourn her loss; and such constancy they seek, by this pretty custom, to commend to their wives. They further pledge each other at this time in these words: "Black is the hair that now crowns our heads, yet when it has become as white as the fibres of the onion root, we shall still be found faithful to each other."

The white heron seems to be the especial friend of man. Many are the tales told of the assistance it has rendered individuals. In one case the generous-hearted creature is said to have pecked off its bill in its frantic attempts to ring a temple bell for the salvation of a man. One of the early stories relates how a hunter, having shot an arrow through the head of a snake that was about to devour some newly hatched herons, was in turn saved by the mother bird, who pecked to death a snake that had gotten into the man's stomach while he was drinking at a spring. The pecking, further, was so expertly done as not to injure the man.

The swallows are everywhere welcome, while the thievish sparrows are killed as often as possible; the former live in the roofs of the houses, and usually awaken the inmates by their delighted chattering at each recurrence of dawn. A charming story is told of a swallow's rewarding a kind man who had rescued it from a snake and bound up its broken leg. The anecdote is too long to be related in this connection further than to say that the bird gave the man a seed which, being planted, brought him a vast fortune, while a seed given to his wicked brother, who was cruel to the swallows, worked his ruin. The bird held in the highest favor, however, is the stork. It is engraved in jade and gold and embroidered in silk, as the insignia of rank for the nobility. It is the bird that soars above the battle, and calls down success upon the Korean arms. In its majestic flight it is supposed to mount to heaven; hence its wisdom, for it is reputed to be a very wise bird. A man was once said to have ridden to heaven on the back of a huge stork, and judging from the great strength of a pair the writer once had as pets, the people are warranted in believing that, in the marvellous days of the ancients, these birds were used for purposes of transportation.

The animals, too, have their stories, and in Korea, as in some other parts of the world, the rabbit seems to come off best, as a rule. One very good story is told concerning a scrape the rabbit got himself into because of his curiosity, but out of which he extricated himself at the expense of the whole fraternity of water animals.

It seems that on one occasion the king of fishes was a little indiscreet, and while snapping greedily at a worm, got a hook through his nose. He succeeded in breaking the line, and escaped having his royal bones picked by some hungry mortal, but he was still in a great dilemma, for he could in no way remove the cruel hook.

His finny majesty grew very ill; all the officials of his kingdom were summoned and met in solemn council. From the turtle to the whale, each one wore an anxious expression, and did his best at thinking. At last the turtle was asked for his opinion, and announced his firm belief that a poultice made from the fresh eye of a rabbit would remove the disorder of their sovereign at once. He was listened to attentively, but his plan was conceded to be impracticable, since they had no fresh rabbit eyes or any means of obtaining them. Then the turtle again came to the rescue, and said that he had a passing acquaintance with the rabbit, whom he had occasionally seen when walking along the beach, and that he would endeavor to bring him to the palace, if the doctors would then take charge of the work, for the sight of blood disagreed with him, and he would ask to absent himself from the further conduct of the case. He was royally thanked for his offer, and sent off in haste, realizing full well that his career was made in case he succeeded, while he would be very much unmade if he failed.

'Twas a very hot day as the fat turtle dragged himself up the hill-side, where he fortunately espied the rabbit. The latter, having jumped away a short distance, cocked his ears, and looked over his back to see who was approaching. Perceiving the turtle, he went over and accosted him with, "What are you doing away up here, sir?"

"I simply came up for a view. I have always heard that the view over the water from your hills was excellent, but I can't say it pays one for the trouble of coming up," and the turtle wiped off his long neck and stretched himself out to cool off in the air.

"You are not high enough; just come with me if you want to see a view," and the rabbit straightened up as if to start.

"No, indeed! I have had enough for once. I prefer the water. Why, you should see the magnificent sights down there. There are beautiful green forests of waving trees, mountains of cool stones, valleys and caves, great open plains made beautiful by companies of brightly robed fishes, royal processions from our palaces, and, best of all, the water bears you up, and you go everywhere without exertion. No, let me return, you have nothing on this dry, hot earth worth seeing." The turtle turned to go, but the rabbit musingly followed. At length he said:

"Don't you have any difficulty in the water? Doesn't it get into your eyes and mouth?" For he really longed in his heart to see the strange sights.

"Oh, no! it bothers us no more than air, after we have once become accustomed to it," said the turtle.

"I should very much like to see the place," said the rabbit, rather to himself, "but 'tis no use, I couldn't live in the water like a fish."

"Why, certainly not," and the turtle concealed his excitement under an air of indifference; "you couldn't get along by yourself, but if you really wish to see something that will surprise you, you may get on my back, give me your fore-paws, and I will take you down all right."

After some further assurance, the rabbit accepted the apparently generous offer, and on arriving at the beach, he allowed himself to be firmly fixed on the turtle's back, and down they went into the water, to the great discomfort of the rabbit, who, however, eventually became so accustomed to the water that he did not much mind it.

He was charmed and bewildered by the magnificence of every thing he saw, and especially by the gorgeous palace, through which he was escorted, by attendant fishes, to the sick chamber of the king, where he found a great council of learned doctors, who welcomed him *very* warmly. While sitting in an elegant chair and gazing about at the surrounding magnificence, he chanced to hear a discussion concerning the best way of securing his eyes before he should die. He was filled with horror, and, questioning an attendant, the whole plot was explained to him. The poor fellow scratched his head and wondered if he would ever get out of the place alive. At last a happy thought struck him. He explained to them that he always carried about two pairs of eyes, his real ones and a pair made of mountain crystals, to be used in very dusty weather.

Fearing that the water would injure his real eyes, he had buried them in the sand before getting upon the turtle's back, and was now using his crystal ones. He further expressed himself as most willing to let them have *one* of his real eyes, with which to cure his majesty's disorder, and assured them that he believed one eye would answer the purpose. He gave them to understand that he felt highly honored in being allowed to assist in so important a work, and declared that if they would give the necessary order he would hasten on the turtle's back to the spot where he had buried the eyes and return speedily with one.

Marvelling much at the rabbit's courtesy, the fishes slunk away into the corners for very shame at their own rude conduct in forcibly kidnapping him, when a simple request would have accomplished their purpose. The turtle was rather roughly commanded to carry the guest to the place designated, which he did.

Once released by the turtle to dig for the eyes in the sand, the rabbit shook the water from his coat, and winking at his clumsy betrayer told him to dig for the eyes himself, that he had only one pair, and those he intended to keep. With that he tore away up the mountain side, and has ever after been careful to give the turtle a wide berth.

THE ENCHANTED WINE-JUG OR, WHY THE CAT AND DOG ARE ENEMIES

In ancient times there lived an old gray-haired man by the river's bank where the ferry-boats land. He was poor but honest, and being childless, and compelled to earn his own food, he kept a little wine-shop, which, small though it was, possessed quite a local reputation, for the aged proprietor would permit no quarrelling on his premises, and sold only one brand of wine, and this was of really excellent quality. He did not keep a pot of broth simmering over the coals at his door to tempt the passer-by, and thus increase his thirst on leaving. The old man rather preferred the customers who brought their little long-necked bottles, and carried the drink to their homes. There were some peculiarities—almost mysteries—about this little wine-shop; the old man had apparently always been there, and had never seemed any younger. His wine never gave out, no matter how great might be the local thirst, yet he was never seen to make or take in a new supply; nor had he a great array of vessels in his shop. On the contrary, he always seemed to pour the wine out of the one and same old bottle, the long, slender neck of which was black and shiny from being so often tipped in his old hand while the generous, warming stream gurgled outward to the bowl. This had long ceased to be a matter of inquiry, however, and only upon the advent of a stranger of an inquiring mind would the subject be re-discussed. The neighbors were assured that the old man was thoroughly good, and that his wine was better. Furthermore, he sold it as reasonably as other men sold a much inferior article. And more than this, they did not care to know; or at least if they did once care, they had gotten over it, and were now content to let well enough alone.

I said the old man had no children. That is true, yet he had that which in a slight degree took the place of children, in that they were his daily care, his constant companions, and the partners of his bed and board. These deputy children were none other than a good-natured old dog, with laughing face and eyes, long silken ears that were ever on the alert, yet too soft to stand erect, a chunky neck, and a large round body covered with long soft tan hair and ending in a bushy tail. He was the very impersonation of canine wisdom and good-nature, and seldom became ruffled unless he saw his master worried by the ill behavior of one of his patrons, or when a festive flea persisted in attacking him on all sides at once. His fellow, a cat, would sometimes assist in the onslaught, when the dog was about to be defeated and completely ruffled by his tormentor.

This "Thomas" was also a character in his own way, and though past the days when his chief ambition had been to catch his tail, he had such a strong vein of humor running through him that age could not subdue his frivolous propensities. He had been known to drop a dead mouse upon the dog's nose from the counter, while the latter was endeavoring to get a quiet nap; and then he would blow his tail up as a balloon, hump his back, and look utterly shocked at such conduct, as the startled dog nearly jumped out of his skin, and growling horribly, tore around as though he were either in chase of a wild beast or being chased by one.

This happy couple lived in the greatest contentment with the old man. They slept in the little *kang* room with him at night, and enjoyed the warm stone floor, with its slick oil-paper covering, as much as did their master. When the old man would go out on a mild moonlit night to enjoy a pipe of tobacco and gaze at the stars, his companions would rush out and announce to the world that they were not asleep, but ready to encounter any and every thing that the darkness might bring forth, so long as it did not enter their master's private court, of which they were in possession.

These two were fair-weather companions up to this time. They had not been with the old man when a bowl of rice was a luxury. Their days did not antedate the period of the successful wine-shop history. The old man, however, often recalled those former days with a shudder, and thought with great complacency of the time when he had befriended a divine being, in the form of a weary human traveller, to whom he gave the last drink his jug contained, and how, when the contents of the little jug had gurgled down the stranger's throat in a long unbroken draught, the stranger had given him a trifling little thing that looked like a bit of amber, saying: "Drop this into your jug, old man, and so long as it remains there, you will never want for a drink." He did so; and sure enough the jug was heavy with something, so that he raised it to his lips, and—could he believe it! a most delicious stream of wine poured down his parched throat.

He took the jug down and peered into its black depths; he shook its sides, causing the elf within to dance and laugh aloud; and shutting his eyes, again he took another long draught; then meaning well, he remembered the stranger, and was about to offer him a drink, when he discovered that he was all alone, and began to wonder at the strange circumstance, and to think what he was to do. "I can't sit here and drink all the time, or I will be drunk, and some thief will carry away my jug. I can't live on wine alone, yet I dare not leave this strange thing while I seek for work."

Like many another to whom fortune has just come, he knew not for a time what to do with his good-luck. Finally he hit upon the scheme of keeping a wine-shop, the success of which we have seen, and have perhaps refused the old man credit for the wisdom he displayed in continuing on in a small scale, rather than in exciting unpleasant curiosity and official oppression, by turning up his jug and attempting to produce wine at wholesale. The dog and cat knew the secret, and had ever a watchful eye upon the jug, which was never for a moment out of sight of one of the three pairs of eyes.

As the brightest day must end in gloom, however, so was this pleasant state soon to be marred by a most sad and far-reaching accident.

One day the news flashed around the neighborhood that the old man's supply of wine was exhausted; not a drop remained in his jug, and he had no more with which to refill it. Each man on hearing the news ran to see if it were indeed true, and the little straw-thatched hut and its small court encircled by a mud wall were soon filled with anxious seekers after the truth. The old man admitted the statement to be true, but had little to say; while the dog's ears hung neglectedly over his cheeks, his eyes dropped, and he looked as though he might be asleep, but for the persistent manner in which he refused to lie down, but dignifiedly bore his portion of the sorrow sitting upright, but with bowed head.

"Thomas" seemed to have been charged with agitation enough for the whole family. He walked nervously about the floor till he felt that justice to his tail demanded a higher plane, where shoes could not offend, and then betook himself to the counter, and later to the beam which supported the roof, and made a sort of cats' and rats' attic under the thatch.

All condoled with the old man, and not one but regretted that their supply of cheap, good wine was exhausted. The old man offered no explanation, though he had about concluded in his own mind that, as no one knew the secret, he must have in some way poured the bit of amber into a customer's jug. But who possessed the jug he could not surmise, nor could he think of any way of reclaiming it. He talked the matter over carefully and fully to himself at night, and the dog and cat listened attentively, winking knowingly at each other, and puzzling their brains much as to what was to be done and how they were to assist their kind old friend.

At last the old man fell asleep, and then sitting down face to face by his side, the dog and cat began a discussion. "I am sure," says the cat, "that I can detect that thing if I only come within smelling distance of it; but how do we know where to look for it." That was a puzzler, but the dog proposed that they make a search through every house in the neighborhood. "We can go on a mere *kuh kyung* (look see), you know, and while you call on the cats indoors, and keep your smellers open, I will *yay gee* (chat) with the dogs outside, and if you smell any thing you can tell me."

The plan seemed to be the only good one, and it was adopted that very night. They were not cast down because the first search was unsuccessful, and continued their work night after night. Sometimes their calls were not appreciated, and in a few cases they had to clear the field by battle before they could go on with the search. No house was neglected, however, and in due time they had done the whole neighborhood, but with no success. They then determined that it must have been carried to the other side of the river, to which place they decided to extend their search as soon as the water was frozen over, so that they could cross on the ice, for they knew they would not be allowed in the crowded ferry-boats; and while the dog could swim, he knew that the water was too icy for that. As it soon grew very cold, the river froze so solidly that bull-carts, ponies, and all passed over on the ice, and so it remained for near two months, allowing the searching party to return each morning to their poor old master, who seemed completely broken up by his loss, and did not venture away from his door, except to buy the few provisions which his little fund of savings would allow.

Time flew by without bringing success to the faithful comrades, and the old man began to think they too were deserting him, as his old customers had done. It was nearing the time for the spring thaw and freshet, when one night as the cat was chasing around over the roof timbers, in a house away to the outside of the settlement across the river, he detected an odor that caused him to stop so suddenly as to nearly precipitate himself upon a sleeping man on the floor below. He carefully traced up the odor, and found that it came from a soapstone tobacco box that sat upon the top of a high clothes-press near by. The box was dusty with neglect, and "Thomas" concluded that the possessor had accidentally turned the

coveted gem (for it was from that the odor came) out into his wine
bowl, and, not knowing its nature, had put it into this stone box
rather than throw it away. The lid was so securely fastened that the
box seemed to be one solid piece, and in despair of opening it, the
cat went out to consult the superior wisdom of the dog, and see
what could be done. "I can't get up there," said the dog, "nor can
you bring me the box, or I might break it."

"I cannot move the thing, or I might push it off, and let it fall to
the floor and break," said the cat.

So after explaining the things they could not do, the dog finally
hit upon a plan they might perhaps successfully carry out. "I will
tell you," said he. "You go and see the chief of the rat guild in
this neighborhood, tell him that if he will help you in this matter,
we will both let him alone for ten years, and not hurt even a
mouse of them."

"But what good is that going to do?"

"Why, don't you see, that stone is no harder than some wood,
and they can take turns at it till they gnaw a hole through, then we
can easily get the gem."

The cat bowed before the marvellous judgment of the dog, and
went off to accomplish the somewhat difficult task of obtaining
an interview with the master rat. Meanwhile the dog wagged his
ears and tail, and strode about with a swinging stride, in imitation
of the great *yang ban*, or official, who occasionally walked past his
master's door, and who seemed to denote by his haughty gait his
superiority to other men. His importance made him impudent, and
when the cat returned, to his dismay, he found his friend engaged
in a genuine fight with a lot of curs who had dared to intrude upon
his period of self-congratulation. "Thomas" mounted the nearest
wall, and howled so lustily that the inmates of the house, awakened
by the uproar, came out and dispersed the contestants.

The cat had found the rat, who, upon being assured of safety,
came to the mouth of his hole, and listened attentively to the

proposition. It is needless to say he accepted it, and a contract was made forthwith. It was arranged that work was to begin at once, and be continued by relays as long as they could work undisturbed, and when the box was perforated, the cat was to be summoned.

The ice had now broken up and the pair could not return home very easily, so they waited about the neighborhood for some months, picking up a scant living, and making many friends and not a few enemies, for they were a proud pair, and ready to fight on provocation.

It was warm weather, when, one night, the cat almost forgot his compact as he saw a big fat rat slinking along towards him. He crouched low and dug his long claws into the earth, while every nerve seemed on the jump; but before he was ready to spring upon his prey, he fortunately remembered his contract. It was just in time, too, for as the rat was none other than the other party to the contract, such a mistake at that time would have been fatal to their object.

The rat announced that the hole was completed, but was so small at the inside end that they were at a loss to know how to get the gem out, unless the cat could reach it with his paw. Having acquainted the dog with the good news, the cat hurried off to see for himself. He could introduce his paw, but as the object was at the other end of the box he could not quite reach it. They were in a dilemma, and were about to give up, when the cat went again to consult with the dog. The latter promptly told them to put a mouse into the box, and let him bring out the gem. They did so, but the hole was too small for the little fellow and his load to get out at the same time, so that much pushing and pulling had to be done before they were successful. They got it safely at last, however, and gave it at once to the dog for safe-keeping. Then, with much purring and wagging of tails, the contract of friendship was again renewed, and the strange party broke up; the rats to go and jubilate over their safety, the dog and cat to carry the good news to their mourning master.

Again canine wisdom was called into play in devising a means for crossing the river. The now happy dog was equal to such a trifling thing as this, however, and instructed the cat that he must take the gem in his mouth, hold it well between his teeth, and then mount his (the dog's) back, where he could hold on firmly to the long hair of his neck while he swam across the river. This was agreed upon, and arriving at the river they put the plan into execution. All went well until, as they neared the opposite bank, a party of school-children chanced to notice them coming, and, after their amazement at the strange sight wore away, they burst into uproarious laughter, which increased the more they looked at the absurd sight. They clapped their hands and danced with glee, while some fell on the ground and rolled about in an exhaustion of merriment at seeing a cat astride a dog's back being ferried across the river.

The dog was too weary, and consequently matter-of-fact, to see much fun in it, but the cat shook his sides till his agitation caused the dog to take in great gulps of water in attempting to keep his head up. This but increased the cat's merriment, till he broke out in a laugh as hearty as that of the children, and in doing so dropped the precious gem into the water. The dog, seeing the sad accident, dove at once for the gem; regardless of the cat, who could not let go in time to escape, and was dragged down under the water. Sticking his claws into the dog's skin, in his agony of suffocation, he caused him so much pain that he missed the object of his search, and came to the surface.

The cat got ashore in some way, greatly angered at the dog's rude conduct. The latter, however, cared little for that, and as soon as he had shaken the water from his hide, he made a lunge at his unlucky companion, who had lost the results of a half year's faithful work in one moment of foolishness.

Dripping like a "drowned cat," "Thomas" was, however, able to climb a tree, and there he stayed till the sun had dried the water from his fur, and he had spat the water from his inwards in the constant spitting he kept up at his now enemy, who kept barking ferociously about the tree below. The cat knew that the dog was dangerous when aroused, and was careful not to descend from his perch till the coast was clear; though at one time he really feared the ugly boys would knock him off with stones as they passed. Once down, he has ever since been careful to avoid the dog, with whom he has never patched up the quarrel. Nor does he wish to do so, for the very sight of a dog causes him to recall that horrible cold ducking and the day spent up a tree, and involuntarily he spits as though still filled with river-water, and his tail blows up as it had never learned to do till the day when for so long its damp and draggled condition would not permit of its assuming the haughty shape. This accounts for the scarcity of cats and the popularity of dogs.[2]

The dog did not give up his efforts even now. He dove many times in vain, and spent most of the following days sitting on the river's bank, apparently lost in thought. Thus the winter found him—his two chief aims apparently being to find the gem and to kill the cat. The latter kept well out of his way, and the ice now covered the place where the former lay hidden. One day he espied a man spearing fish through a hole in the ice, as was very common. Having a natural desire to be around where any thing eatable was being displayed, and feeling a sort of proprietorship in the particular part of the river where the man was fishing, and where he himself had had such a sad experience, he went down and looked on. As a fish came up, something natural seemed to greet his nostrils, and then, as the man lay down his catch, the dog grabbed it and rushed off in the greatest haste. He ran with all his might to his master, who, poor man, was now at the end of his string (coin in Korea is perforated and strung on a string), and was almost reduced to begging. He was therefore delighted when his faithful old friend brought him so acceptable a present as a fresh fish. He at once commenced dressing it, but when

---

2. Cats are indeed rare in Korea, while dogs are as abundant as in Constantinople.

he slit it open, to his infinite joy, his long-lost gem fell out of the fish's belly. The dog was too happy to contain himself, but jumping upon his master, he licked him with his tongue, and struck him with his paws, barking meanwhile as though he had again treed the cat.

As soon as their joy had become somewhat natural, the old man carefully placed the gem in his trunk, from which he took the last money he had, together with some fine clothes—relics of his more fortunate days. He had feared he must soon pawn these clothes, and had even shown them to the brokers. But now he took them out to put them on, as his fortune had returned to him. Leaving the fish baking on the coals, he donned his fine clothes, and taking his last money, he went and purchased wine for his feast, and for a beginning; for he knew that once he placed the gem back in the jug, the supply of wine would not cease. On his return he and the good dog made a happy feast of the generous fish, and the old man completely recovered his spirits when he had quaffed deeply of the familiar liquid to which his mouth was now such a stranger. Going to his trunk directly, he found to his amazement that it contained another suit of clothes exactly like the first ones he had removed, while there lay also a broken string of cash of just the amount which he had previously taken out.

Sitting down to think, the whole truth dawned upon him, and he then saw how he had abused his privilege before in being content to use his talisman simply to run a wine-shop, while he might have had money and every thing else in abundance by simply giving the charm a chance to work.

Acting upon this principle, the old man eventually became immensely wealthy, for he could always duplicate any thing with his piece of amber. He carefully tended his faithful dog, who never in his remaining days molested a rat, and never lost an opportunity to attack every cat he saw.

CHING YUH AND KYAIN OO THE TRIALS OF TWO HEAVENLY LOVERS

PRELUDE

Ching Yuh and Kyain Oo were stars attendant upon the Sun. They fell madly in love with each other, and, obtaining the royal permission, they were married. It was to them a most happy union, and having reached the consummation of their joys they lived only for one another, and sought only each other's company. They were continually in each other's embrace, and as the honeymoon bade fair to continue during the rest of their lives, rendering them unfit for the discharge of their duties, their master decided to punish them. He therefore banished them, one to the farthest edge of the eastern heavens, the other to the extreme opposite side of the great river that divides the heavenly plains (the Milky Way).

They were sent so far away that it required full six months to make the journey, or a whole year to go and come. As they must be at their post at the annual inspection, they therefore could only hope to journey back and forth for the scant comfort of spending one short night in each other's company. Even should they violate their orders and risk punishment by returning sooner, they could only see each other from either bank of the broad river, which they could only hope to cross at the season when the great bridge is completed by the crows, who carry the materials for its construction upon their heads, as any one may know, who cares to notice, how bald and worn are the heads of the crows during the seventh moon.

Naturally this fond couple are always heart-broken and discouraged at being so soon compelled to part after such a brief but long-deferred meeting, and 'tis not strange that their grief should manifest itself in weeping tears so copious that the whole earth beneath is deluged with rains.

This sad meeting occurs on the night of the seventh day of the seventh moon, unless prevented by some untoward circumstance, in which case the usual rainy season is withheld, and the parched earth then unites in lamentation with the fond lovers, whose increased trials so sadden their hearts that even the fountain of tears refuses to flow for their relief.

I.

You Tah Jung was a very wise official, and a remarkably good man. He could ill endure the corrupt practices of many of his associate officials, and becoming dissatisfied with life at court, he sought and obtained permission to retire from official life and go to the country. His marriage had fortunately been a happy one, hence he was the more content with the somewhat solitary life he now began to lead. His wife was peculiarly gifted, and they were in perfect sympathy with each other, so that they longed not for the society of others. They had one desire, however, that was ever before them and that could not be laid aside. They had no children; not even a daughter had been granted them.

As You Tah Jung superintended the cultivation of his estate, he felt that he would be wholly happy and content were it not for the lack of offspring. He gave himself up to the fascinating pastime of fishing, and took great delight in spending the most of his time in the fields listening to the birds and absorbing wisdom, with peace and contentment, from nature. As spring brought the mating and budding season, however, he again got to brooding over his unfortunate condition. For as he was the last of an illustrious family, the line seemed like to cease with his childless life. He knew of the displeasure his ancestors would experience, and that he would be unable to face them in paradise; while he would leave no one to bow before his grave and make offerings to his spirit. Again he bemoaned their condition with his poor wife, who begged him to avail himself of his prerogative and remove their reproach by marrying another wife. This he stoutly refused to do, as he would not risk ruining his now pleasant home by bringing another wife and the usual discord into it.

Instead of estranging them, their misfortune seemed but to bind this pair the closer together. They were very devout people, and they prayed to heaven continually for a son. One night the wife fell asleep while praying, and dreamed a remarkable dream. She fancied that she saw a commotion in the vicinity of the North Star, and presently a most beautiful boy came down to her, riding upon a wonderful fan made of white feathers. The boy came direct to her and made a low obeisance, upon which she asked him who he was and where he came from. He said: "I am the attendant of the great North Star, and because of a mistake I fell into he banished me to earth for a term of years, telling me to come to you and bring this fan, which will eventually be the means of saving your life and my own."

In the intensity of her joy she awoke, and found to her infinite sorrow that the beautiful vision was but a dream. She cherished it in her mind, however, and was transported with joy when a beautiful boy came to them with the succeeding spring-tide. The beauty of the child was the comment of the neighborhood, and every one loved him. As he grew older it was noticed that the graces of his mind were even more remarkable than those of his person.

The next ten years were simply one unending period of blissful contentment in the happy country home. They called the boy Pang Noo (his family name being You, made him You Pang Noo). His mother taught him his early lessons herself, but by the expiration of his first ten years he had grown far beyond her powers, and his brilliant mind even taxed his intelligent father in his attempts to keep pace with him.

About this time they learned of a wonderful teacher, a Mr. Nam Juh Oon, whose ability was of great repute. It was decided that the boy should be sent to this man to school, and great was the agitation and sorrow at home at thought of the separation. He was made ready, however, and with the benediction of father and caresses of mother, he started for his new teacher, bearing with him a wonderful feather fan which his father had given him, and which had descended from his great-grandfather. This he was to guard with especial care, as, since his mother's remarkable dream, preceding his birth, it was believed that this old family relic, which bore such a likeness to the fan of the dream, was to prove a talisman to him, and by it evil was to be warded off, and good brought down upon him.

II.

Strange as it may seem, events very similar in nature to those just narrated were taking place in a neighboring district, where lived another exemplary man named Cho Sung Noo. He was a man of great rank, but was not in active service at present, simply because of ill-health induced by constant brooding over his ill-fortune; for, like You Tah Jung, he was the last of an illustrious family, and had no offspring. He was so happily married, furthermore, that he had never taken a second wife, and would not do so.

About the time of the events just related concerning the You family, the wife of Cho, who had never neglected bowing to heaven and requesting a child, dreamed. She had gone to a hill-side apart from the house, and sitting in the moonlight on a clean plat of ground, free from the litter of the domestic animals, she was gazing into the heavens, hoping to witness the meeting of *Ching Yuh* and *Kyain Oo*, and feeling sad at the thought of their fabled tribulations. While thus engaged she fell asleep, and while sleeping dreamed that the four winds were bearing to her a beautiful litter, supported upon five rich, soft clouds. In the chair reclined a beautiful little girl, far lovelier than any being she had ever dreamed of before, and the like of which is never seen in real life. The chair itself was made of gold and jade. As the procession drew nearer the dreamer exclaimed: "Who are you, my beautiful child?"

"Oh," replied the child, "I am glad you think me beautiful, for then, may be, you will let me stay with you."

"I think I should like to have you very much, but you haven't yet answered my question."

"Well," she said, "I was an attendant upon the Queen of Heaven, but I have been very bad, though I meant no wrong, and I am banished to earth for a season; won't you let me live with you, please?"

"I shall be delighted, my child, for we have no children. But what did you do that the stars should banish you from their midst?"

"Well, I will tell you," she answered. "You see, when the annual union of Ching Yuh and Kyain Oo takes place, I hear them mourning because they can only see each other once a year, while mortal pairs have each other's company constantly. They never consider that while mortals have but eighty years of life at most, their lives are without limit, and they, therefore, have each other to a greater extent than do the mortals, whom they selfishly envy. In a spirit of mischief I determined to teach this unhappy couple a lesson; consequently, on the last seventh moon, seventh day, when the bridge was about completed and ready for the eager pair to cross heaven's river to each others' embrace, I drove the crows away, and ruined their bridge before they could reach each other. I did it for mischief, 'tis true, and did not count on the drought that would occur, but for my misconduct and the consequent suffering entailed on mortals, I am banished, and I trust you will take and care for me, kind lady."

When she had finished speaking, the winds began to blow around as though in preparation for departure with the chair, minus its occupant. Then the woman awoke and found it but a dream, though the winds were, indeed, blowing about her so as to cause her to feel quite chilly. The dream left a pleasant impression, and when, to their intense joy, a daughter was really born to them, the fond parents could scarcely be blamed for associating her somewhat with the vision of the ravishing dream.

The child was a marvel of beauty, and her development was rapid and perfect. The neighbors were so charmed with her, that some of them seemed to think she was really supernatural, and she was popularly known as the "divine maiden," before her first ten years were finished.

It was about the time of her tenth birthday that little Uhn Hah had the interesting encounter upon which her whole future was to hinge.

It happened in this way: One day she was riding along on her nurses' back, on her way to visit her grandmother. Coming to a nice shady spot they sat down by the road-side to rest. While they were sitting there, along came Pang Noo on his way to school. As Uhn Hah was still but a girl she was not veiled, and the lad was confronted with her matchless beauty, which seemed to intoxicate him. He could not pass by, neither could he find words to utter, but at last he bethought him of an expedient. Seeing some oranges in her lap, he stepped up and spoke politely to the nurse, saying, "I am You Pang Noo, a lad on my way to school, and I am very thirsty, won't you ask your little girl to let me have one of her oranges?" Uhn Hah was likewise smitten with the charms of the beautiful lad, and in her confusion she gave him two oranges. Pang Noo gallantly said, "I wish to give you something in return for your kindness, and if you will allow me I will write your name on this fan and present it to you."

Having obtained the name and permission, he wrote: "No girl was ever possessed of such incomparable graces as the beautiful Uhn Hah. I now betroth myself to her, and vow never to marry other so long as I live." He handed her the fan, and feasting his eyes on her beauty, they separated. The fan being closed, no one read the characters, and Uhn Hah carefully put it away for safe keeping without examining it sufficiently close to discover the written sentiment.

III.

Pang Noo went to school and worked steadily for three years. He learned amazingly fast, and did far more in three years than the brightest pupils usually do in ten. His noted teacher soon found that the boy could even lead him, and it became evident that further stay at the school was unnecessary. The boy also was very anxious to go and see his parents. At last he bade his teacher good-by, to the sorrow of both, for their companionship had been very pleasant and profitable, and they had more than the usual attachment of teacher and pupil for each other. Pang Noo and his attendant journeyed leisurely to their home, where they were received with the greatest delight. His mother had not seen her son during his schooling, and even her fond pride was hardly prepared for the great improvement the boy had made, both in body and mind, since last she saw him. The father eventually asked to see the ancestral fan he had given him, and the boy had to confess that he had it not, giving as an excuse that he had lost it on the road. His father could not conceal his anger, and for some time their pleasure was marred by this unfortunate circumstance. Such a youth and an only son could not long remain unforgiven, however, and soon all was forgotten, and he enjoyed the fullest love of his parents and admiration of his friends as he quietly pursued his studies and recreation.

In this way he came down to his sixteenth year, the pride of the neighborhood. His quiet was remarked, but no one knew the secret cause, and how much of his apparent studious attention was devoted to the charming little maiden image that was framed in his mental vision. About this time a very great official from the neighborhood called upon his father, and after the usual formalities, announced that he had heard of the remarkable son You Tah Jung was the father of, and he had come to consult upon the advisability of uniting their families, as he himself had been blessed with a daughter who was beautiful and accomplished. You Tah Jung was delighted at the prospect of making such a fine alliance for his son, and gave his immediate consent, but to his dismay, his son objected so strenuously and withal so honorably that the proposition had to be declined as graciously as the rather awkward circumstances would allow. Both men being sensible, however, they but admired the boy the more, for the clever rascal had begged his father to postpone all matrimonial matters, as far as he was concerned, till he had been able to make a name for himself, and had secured rank, that he might merit such attention.

Pang Noo was soon to have an opportunity to distinguish himself. A great *quaga* (civil-service examination) was to be held at the capital, and Pang Noo announced his intention of entering the lists and competing for civil rank. His father was glad, and in due time started him off in proper style. The examination was held in a great enclosure at the rear of the palace, where the King and his counsellors sat in a pavilion upon a raised stage of masonry. The hundreds of men and youths from all parts of the country were seated upon the ground under large umbrellas. Pang Noo was given a subject, and soon finished his essay, after which he folded it up carefully and tossed the manuscript over a wall into an enclosure, where it was received and delivered to the board of examiners. These gentlemen, as well as His Majesty, were at once struck with the rare merit of the production, and made instant inquiry concerning the writer. Of course he was successful, and a herald soon announced that Pang, the son of You Tah Jung had taken the highest honors. He was summoned before the King, who was pleased with the young man's brightness and wisdom. In addition to his own rank, his father was made governor of a province, and made haste to come to court and thank his sovereign for the double honor, and to congratulate his son.

Pang was given permission to go and bow at the tomb of his ancestors, in grateful acknowledgment for Heaven's blessings. Having done which, he went to pay his respects to his mother, who fairly worshipped her son now, if she had not done so before. During his absence the King had authorized the board of appointments to give him the high rank of *Ussa*, for, though he was young, His Majesty thought one so wise and quick, well fitted to travel in disguise and spy out the acts of evil officials, learn the condition of the people, and bring the corrupt and usurous to punishment. Pang Noo was amazed at his success, yet the position just suited him, for, aside from a desire to better the condition of his fellow-men, he felt that in this position he would be apt to learn the whereabouts of his lady-love, whose beautiful vision was ever before him. Donning a suitable disguise, therefore, he set out upon the business at hand with a light heart.

IV.

Uhn Hah during all this time had been progressing in a quiet way as a girl should, but she also was quite the wonder of her neighborhood. All this time she had had many, if not constant, dreams of the handsome youth she had met by the roadside. She had lived over the incident time and again, and many a time did she take down and gaze upon the beautiful fan, which, however, opened and closed in such a manner that, ordinarily, the characters were concealed. At last, however, she discovered them, and great was her surprise and delight at the message. She dwelt on it much, and finally concluded it was a heaven arranged union, and as the lad had pledged his faith to her, she vowed she would be his, or never marry at all. This thought she nourished, longing to see Pang Noo, and wondering how she should ever find him, till she began to regard herself as really the wife of her lover.

About this time one of His Majesty's greatest generals, who had a reputation for bravery and cruelty as well, came to stop at his country holding near by, and hearing of the remarkable girl, daughter of the retired, but very honorable, brother official, he made a call at the house of Mr. Cho, and explained that he was willing to betroth his son to Cho's daughter. The matter was considered at length, and Cho gave his willing consent. Upon the departure of the General, the father went to acquaint his daughter with her good fortune. Upon hearing it, she seemed struck dumb, and then began to weep and moan, as though some great calamity had befallen her. She could say nothing, nor bear to hear any more said of the matter. She could neither eat nor sleep, and the roses fled from her tear-bedewed cheeks. Her parents were dismayed, but wisely abstained from troubling her. Her mother, however, betimes lovingly coaxed her daughter to confide in her, but it was long before the girl could bring herself to disclose a secret so peculiar and apparently so unwomanly. The mother prevailed at last, and the whole story of the early infatuation eventually came forth. "He has pledged himself to me," she said, "he recognized me at sight as his heaven-sent bride, and I have pledged myself to him. I cannot marry another, and, should I never find him on earth, this fan shall be my husband till death liberates my spirit to join his in the skies." She enumerated his great charms of manner and person, and begged her mother not to press this other marriage upon her, but rather let her die, insisting, however, that should she die her mother must tell Pang Noo how true she had been to him.

The father was in a great dilemma. "Why did you not tell this to your mother before? Here the General has done me the honor to ask that our families be united, and I have consented. Now I must decline, and his anger will be so great that he will ruin me at the Capitol. And then, after all, this is but an absurd piece of childish foolishness. Your fine young man, had he half the graces you give him, would have been betrothed long before this."

"No! No!" she exclaimed, "he has pledged himself, and I know he is even now coming to me. He will not marry another, nor can I. Would you ask one woman to marry two men? Yet that is what you ask in this, for I am already the wife of Pang Noo in my heart. Kill me, if you will, but spare me this, I beg and entreat," and she writhed about on her cot, crying till the mat was saturated with her tears.

The parents loved her too well to withstand her pleadings, and resigning themselves to the inevitable persecution that must result, they dispatched a letter to the General declining his kind offer, in as unobjectionable a manner as possible. It had the result that was feared. The General, in a towering rage, sent soldiers to arrest Mr. Cho, but before he could go further, a messenger arrived from Seoul with despatches summoning him to the Capitol immediately, as a rebellion had broken out on the borders. Before leaving, however, he instructed the local magistrate to imprison the man and not release him till he consented to the marriage. It chanced that the magistrate was an honest man and knew the General to be a very cruel, relentless warrior. He therefore listened to Cho's story, and believed the strange case. Furthermore, his love for the girl softened his heart, and he bade them to collect what they could and go to another province to live. Cho did so, with deep gratitude to the magistrate, while the latter wrote to the General that the prisoner had avoided arrest and fled to unknown parts, taking his family with him.

V.

Poor Pang Noo did his inspection work with a heavy heart as time wore on, and the personal object of his search was not attained. In the course of his travels he finally came to his uncle, the magistrate who had dismissed the Cho family. The uncle welcomed his popular nephew right warmly, but questioned him much as to the cause of his poor health and haggard looks, which so ill-became a man of his youth and prospects. At last the kind old man secured the secret with its whole story, and then it was his turn to be sad, for had he not just sent away the very person the *Ussa* so much desired to see?

When Pang learned this his malady increased, and he declared he could do no more active service till this matter was cleared up.

Consequently he sent a despatch to court begging to be released, as he was in such poor health he could not properly discharge his arduous duties longer. His request was granted, and he journeyed to Seoul, hoping to find some trace of her who more and more seemed to absorb his every thought and ambition.

VI.

In the meantime the banished family, heart-sick and travel-worn, had settled temporarily in a distant hamlet, where the worn and discouraged parents were taken sick. Uhn Hah did all she could for them, but in spite of care and attention, in spite of prayers and tears, they passed on to join their ancestors. The poor girl beat her breast and tore her hair in an agony of despair. Alone in a strange country, with no money and no one to shield and support her, it seemed that she too must, perforce, give up. But her old nurse urged her to cheer up, and suggested their donning male attire, in which disguise they could safely journey to another place unmolested.

The idea seemed a good one, and it was adopted. They allowed their hair to fall down the back in a long braid, after the fashion of the unmarried men, and, putting on men's clothes, they had no trouble in passing unnoticed along the roads. After having gone but a short distance they found themselves near the capital of the province— the home of the Governor. While sitting under some trees by the roadside the Governor's procession passed by. The couple arose respectfully, but the Governor (it was Pang Noo's father), espying the peculiar feather fan, ordered one of the runners to seize the women and bring them along. It was done; and when they were arrived at the official yamen, he questioned the supposed man as to where he had secured that peculiar fan. "It is a family relic," replied Uhn Hah, to the intense amazement of the Governor, who pronounced the statement false, as the fan was a peculiar feature in his own family, and must be one that had descended from his own ancestors and been found or stolen by the present possessor.

However, the Governor offered to pay a good round sum for the fan. But Uhn Hah declared she would die rather than part with it, and the two women in disguise were locked up in prison. A man of clever speech was sent to interview them, and he offered them a considerable sum for the fan, which the servant urged Uhn Hah to take, as they were sadly in want. After the man had departed in disgust, however, the girl upbraided her old nurse roundly for forsaking her in her time of trial. "My parents are dead," she said. "All I have to represent my husband is this fan that I carry in my bosom. Would you rob me of this? Never speak so again if you wish to retain my love"; and, weeping, she fell into the servant's arms, where, exhausted and overwrought nature asserting itself, sleep closed her eyes.

While sleeping she dreamed of a wonderful palace on high, where she saw a company of women, who pointed her to the blood-red reeds that lined the river bank below, explaining that their tears had turned to blood during their long search for their lovers, and dropping on the reeds they were dyed blood-red. One of them prophesied, however, that Uhn Hah was to be given superhuman strength and powers, and that she would soon succeed in finding her lover, who was now a high official, and so true to her that he was sick because he could not find her. She awakened far more refreshed by the dream than by the nap, and was soon delighted by being dismissed. The Governor's steward took pity on the handsome "boy," and gave him a parting gift of wine and food to carry with them, as well as some cash to help them on, and, bidding him good-by, the women announced their intention of travelling to a distant province.

VII.

Meanwhile Pang Noo had reached home, and was weary both in body and mind. The King offered him service at court, but he asked to be excused, and seemed to wish to hide himself and avoid meeting people. His father marvelled much at this, and again urged the young man to marry; but this seemed only to aggravate his complaint. His uncle happened to come to his father's gubernatorial seat on a business errand, and in pity for the young man, explained the cause of the trouble to the father. He saw it all, and recalled the strange beauty of the lad who had risked his life for the possession of the fan, and as the uncle told the story of her excellent parentage, and the trouble and death that resulted from the refusal to marry, he saw through the whole strange train of circumstances, and marvelled that heaven should have selected such an exemplary maiden for his son. And then, as he realized how nearly he had come to punishing her severely, for her persistent refusal to surrender the fan, and that, whereas, he might have retained her and united her to his son, he had sent her away unattended to wander alone; he heaped blame upon the son in no stinted manner for his lack of confidence in not telling his father his troubles. The attendants were carefully questioned concerning the conduct of the strange couple while in custody at the governor's yamen, and as to the probable direction they took in departure. The steward alone could give information. He was well rewarded for having shown them kindness, but his information cast a gloom upon the trio, for he said they had started for the district where civil war was in progress.

"You unnatural son," groaned the father. "What have you done? You secretly pledge yourself to this noble girl, and then, by your foolish silence, twice allow her to escape, while you came near being the cause of her death at the very hands of your father; and even now by your foolishness she is journeying to certain death. Oh, my son! we have not seen the last of this rash conduct; this noble woman's blood will be upon our hands, and you will bring your poor father to ruin and shame. Up! Stop your lovesick idling, and do something. Ask His Majesty, with my consent, for military duty; go to the seat of war, and there find your wife or your honor."

The father's advice was just what was needed; the son could not, of necessity, disobey, nor did he wish to; but arming himself with the courage of a desperate resolve to save his sweetheart, whom he fancied already in danger from the rebels, he hurried to Seoul, and surprising his sovereign by his strange and ardent desire for military service, easily secured the favor, for the general in command was the same who had wished to marry his son to Uhn Hah; he was also an enemy to Pang Noo's father, and would like to see the only son of his enemy killed.

With apparently strange haste the expedition was started off, and no time was lost on the long, hard march. Arriving near the seat of war, the road led by a mountain, where the black weather-worn stone was as bare as a wall, sloping down to the road. Fearing lest he was going to his death, the young commander had some characters cut high on the face of the rock, which read:

"Standing at the gate of war, I, You Pang Noo, humbly bow to Heaven's decree. Is it victory, or is it death? Heaven alone knows the issue. My only remaining desire is to behold the face of my lady Cho Gah." He put this inscription in this conspicuous place, with the hope that if she were in the district she would see it, and not only know he was true to her, but also that she might be able to ascertain his whereabouts and come to him. He met the rebels, and fought with a will, bringing victory to the royal arms. But soon their provisions gave out, and, though daily despatches arrived, no rations were sent in answer to their constant demands. The soldiers sickened and died. Many more, driven mad by hardship and starvation, buried their troubles deep in the silent river, which their loyal spears had stained crimson with their enemies blood.

You Pang Noo was about to retire against orders, when the rebels, emboldened by the weak condition of their adversaries, came in force, conquered and slew the remnant, and would have slain the commander but for the counsel of two of their number, who urged that he be imprisoned and held for ransom.

VIII.

Again fate had interfered to further separate the lovers, for, instead of continuing her journey, Uhn Hah had received news that induced her to start for Seoul. While resting, on one occasion, they had some conversation with a passer-by. He was from the capital, and stated that he had gone there from a place near Uhn Hah's childhood home as an attendant of the *Ussa* You Pang Noo, who had taken sick at his uncle's, the magistrate, and had gone to Seoul, where he was excused from *ussa* duty and offered service at court. He knew not of the recent changes, but told his eager listener all he knew of Pang Noo's family.

The weary, foot-sore girl and her companion turned their faces toward the capital, hoping at last to be rewarded by finding the object of their search. That evening darkness overtook them before they had found shelter, and spying a light through the trees, they sought it out, and found a little hut occupied by an old man. He was reading a book, but laid it aside as they answered his invitation to enter, given in response to their knock. The usual salutations were exchanged, but instead of asking who the visitors were, where they lived, etc., etc., the old man called her by her true name, Cho Nang Jah. "I am not a Nang Jah" (a female appellation), she exclaimed; "I am a man!"

"Oh! I know you, laughed the old man; "you are Cho Nang Jah in very truth, and you are seeking your future husband in this disguise. But you are perfectly safe here."

"Ask me no questions," said he, as she was about to utter some surprised inquiries. "I have been waiting for you and expecting you. You are soon to do great things, for which I will prepare you. Never mind your hunger, but devour this pill; it will give you superhuman strength and courage." He gave her a pill of great size, which she ate, and then fell asleep on the floor. The old man went away, and soon the tired servant slept also. When they awoke it was bright morning, and the birds were singing in the trees above them, which were their only shelter, for the hut of the previous evening had disappeared entirely, as had also the old man. Concluding that the old man must be some heaven-sent messenger, she devoutly bowed herself in grateful acknowledgment of the gracious manifestation.

Journeying on, they soon came to a wayside inn kept by an old farmer, and here they procured food. While they were eating, a blind man was prophesying for the people. When he came to Uhn Hah he said: "This is a woman in disguise; she is seeking for her husband, who is fighting the rebels, and searching for her. He is now nearly dead; but he will not die, for she will rescue him." On hearing this she was delighted and sad at the same time, and explaining some of her history to the master of the house, he took her in with the women and treated her kindly. She was very anxious to be about her work, however, since heaven had apparently so clearly pointed it out to her, and, bidding the simple but kind friends good-by, she started for the seat of war, where she arrived after a long, tedious, but uneventful tramp.

Almost the first thing she saw was the inscription on the rocks left by the very one she sought, and she cried bitterly at the thought that maybe she was too late. The servant cheered her up, however, by reciting the blind man's prophecy, and they went on their way till they came to a miserable little inn, where they secured lodging. After being there some time, Uhn Hah noticed that the innkeeper's wife was very sad, and continually in tears. She therefore questioned her as to the cause of her grief. "I am mourning over the fate of the poor starved soldiers, killed by the neglect of some one at Seoul, and for the brave young officer, You Pang Noo, whom the rebels have carried away captive." At this Uhn Hah fainted away, and the nurse made such explanation as she could. Restoratives were applied, and she slowly recovered, when, on further questioning, it was found that the inn-people were slaves of You Pang Noo, and had followed him thus far. It was also learned that the absence of stores was generally believed to be due to the corrupt general-in-chief, who not only hated his gallant young officer, but was unwilling to let him achieve glory, so long as he could prevent it.

After consultation, and learning further of the matter, Uhn Hah wrote a letter explaining the condition of affairs, and dispatched it to Pang Noo's father by the innkeeper. The Governor was not at his country place, and the messenger had to go to Seoul, where, to his horror, he found that his old master was in prison, sent there by the influence of the corrupt General, his enemy, because his son had been accused of being a traitor, giving over the royal troops to the rebels, and escaping with them himself. The innkeeper, however, secured access to the prison, and delivered the letter to the unfortunate parent. Of course, nothing could be done, and again he blamed his son for his stupid secrecy in concealing his troubles from his father, and thus bringing ruin upon the family and injury to the young lady. However, he wrote a letter to the good uncle, relating the facts, and requesting him to find the girl, place her in his home, and care for her as tenderly as possible. He could do nothing more. The innkeeper delivered this letter to the uncle, and was then instructed to carry a litter and attendants to his home and bring back the young lady, attired in suitable garments. He did so as speedily as possible, though the journey was a long and tedious one.

Once installed in a comfortable home poor Uhn Hah became more and more lonely. She seemed to have nothing now to hope for, and the stagnation of idleness was more than she could endure. She fancied her lover in prison, and suffering, while she was in the midst of comfort and luxury. She could not endure the thought, and prevailed upon her benefactor to convey to His Majesty a petition praying that she be given a body of soldiers and be allowed to go and punish the rebels, reclaim the territory, and liberate her husband. The King marvelled much at such a request, coming from one of her retiring, seclusive sex, and upon the advice of the wicked General, who was still in command, the petition was not granted. Still she persisted, and found other ways of reaching the throne, till the King, out of curiosity to see such a brave and loyal woman, bade her come before him.

When she entered the royal presence her beauty and dignity of carriage at once won attention and respectful admiration, so that her request was about to be granted, when the General suggested, as a last resort, that she first give some evidence of her strength and prowess before the national military reputation be entrusted to her keeping. It seemed a wise thought, and the King asked her what she could do to show that she was warranted in heading such a perilous expedition. She breathed a prayer to her departed parents for help, and remembering the strange promise of the old man who gave her the pill, she felt that she could do almost any thing, and seizing a large weather-worn stone that stood in an ornamental rock basin in the court, she threw it over the enclosing wall as easily as two men would have lifted it from the ground. Then, taking the General's sword, she began slowly to manipulate it, increasing gradually, as though in keeping with hidden music, till the movement became so rapid that the sword seemed like one continuous ring of burning steel—now in the air, now about her own person, and, again, menacingly near the wicked General, who cowered in abject terror before the remarkable sight. His Majesty was completely captivated, and himself gave the orders for her expedition, raising her to relative rank, and giving her the choicest battalion of troops. In her own peculiarly dignified way she expressed her gratitude, and, bowing to the ground, went forth to execute her sovereign's commands, and attain her heart's desire.

Again donning male attire, she completed her preparations, and departed with eager delight to accomplish her mission. The troops having obtained an inkling of the strange character and almost supernatural power of their handsome, dashing leader, were filled with courage and eager for the fray. But to the dismay of all, they had no sooner arrived at the rebel infested country than severe rains began to fall, making it impossible to accomplish any thing. This was explained, however, by the spirits of the departed soldiers, who appeared to the officers in dreams, and announced that as they had been sacrificed by the cruel General, who had intentionally withheld their rations, they would allow no success to the royal arms till their death was avenged by his death. This was dispatched to court, and believed by His Majesty, who had heard similar reports, oft repeated. He therefore confined the General in prison, and sent his son (the one who wished to marry Uhn Hah) to the front to be executed.

He was slain and his blood scattered to the winds. A feast was prepared for the spirits of the departed soldiers, and this sacrifice having been made, the storm ceased, the sun shone, and the royal troops met and completely vanquished the rebels, restoring peace to the troubled districts, but not obtaining the real object of the leaders' search. After much questioning, among the captives, a man was found who knew all about You Pang Noo, and where he was secreted. Upon the promise of pardon, he conducted a party who rescued the captive and brought him before their commander. Of course for a time the lovers could not recognize each other after the years that had elapsed since their first chance meeting.

You Pang Noo was given command and Uhn Hah modestly retired, adopted her proper dress, and was borne back to Seoul in a litter. The whole country rang with their praises. You Pang Noo was appointed governor of a province, and the father was reinstated in office, while the General who had caused the trouble was ignominiously put to death, and his whole family and his estates were confiscated.

As Cho Uhn Hah had no parents, His Majesty determined that she should have royal patronage, and decreed that their wedding should take place in the great hall where the members of the royal family are united in marriage. This was done with all the pomp and circumstance of a royal wedding, and no official stood so high in the estimation of the King, as the valiant, true-hearted You, while the virtues of his spouse were the subject of songs and ballads, and she was extolled as the model for the women of the country.

HYUNG BO AND NAHL BO; OR, THE SWALLOW-KING'S REWARDS.

I.

In the province of Chullado, in Southern Korea, lived two brothers. One was very rich, the other very poor. For in dividing the inheritance, the elder brother, instead of taking the father's place, and providing for the younger children, kept the whole property to himself, allowing his younger brother nothing at all, and reducing him to a condition of abject misery. Both men were married. Nahl Bo, the elder, had many concubines, in addition to his wife, but had no children; while Hyung Bo had but one wife and several children. The former's wives were continually quarrelling; the latter lived in contentment and peace with his wife, each endeavoring to help the other bear the heavy burdens circumstances had placed upon them. The elder brother lived in a fine, large compound, with warm, comfortable houses; the younger had built himself a hut of broom straw, the thatch of which was so poor that when it rained they were deluged inside, upon the earthern floor. The room was so small, too, that when Hyung Bo stretched out his legs in his sleep his feet were apt to be thrust through the wall. They had no *kang*, and had to sleep upon the cold dirt floor, where insects were so abundant as to often succeed in driving the sleepers out of doors.

They had no money for the comforts of life, and were glad when a stroke of good fortune enabled them to obtain the necessities. Hyung Bo worked whenever he could get work, but rainy days and dull seasons were a heavy strain upon them. The wife did plain sewing, and together they made straw sandals for the peasants and vendors. At fair time the sandal business was good, but then came a time when no more food was left in the house, the string for making the sandals was all used up, and they had no money for a new supply. Then the children cried to their mother for food, till her heart ached for them, and the father wandered off in a last attempt to get something to keep the breath of life in his family.

Not a kernel of rice was left. A poor rat which had cast in his lot with this kind family, became desperate when, night after night, he chased around the little house without being able to find the semblance of a meal. Becoming desperate, he vented his despair in such loud squealing that he wakened the neighbors, who declared that the mouse said his legs were worn off running about in a vain search for a grain of rice with which to appease his hunger. The famine became so serious in the little home, that at last the mother commanded her son to go to his uncle and tell him plainly how distressed they were, and ask him to loan them enough rice to subsist on till they could get work, when they would surely return the loan.

The boy did not want to go. His uncle would never recognize him on the street, and he was afraid to go inside his house lest he should whip him. But the mother commanded him to go, and he obeyed. Outside his uncle's house were many cows, well fed and valuable. In pens he saw great fat pigs in abundance, and fowls were everywhere in great numbers. Many dogs also were there, and they ran barking at him, tearing his clothes with their teeth and frightening him so much that he was tempted to run; but speaking kindly to them, they quieted down, and one dog came and licked his hand as if ashamed of the conduct of the others. A female servant ordered him away, but he told her he was her master's nephew, and wanted to see him; whereupon she smiled but let him pass into an inner court, where he found his uncle sitting on the little veranda under the broad, overhanging eaves.

The man gruffly demanded, "who are you?" "I am your brother's son," he said. "We are starving at our house, and have had no food for three days. My father is away now trying to find work, but we are very hungry, and only ask you to loan us a little rice till we can get some to return you."

The uncle's eyes drew down to a point, his brows contracted, and he seemed very angry, so that the nephew began looking for an easy way of escape in case he should come at him. At last he looked up and said: "My rice is locked up, and I have ordered the granaries not to be opened. The flour is sealed and cannot be broken into. If I give you some cold victuals, the dogs will bark at you and try to take it from you. If I give you the leavings of the wine-press, the pigs will be jealous and squeal at you. If I give you bran, the cows and fowls will take after you. Get out, and let me never see you here again." So saying, he caught the poor boy by the collar and threw him into the outer court, hurting him, and causing him to cry bitterly with pain of body and distress of mind.

At home the poor mother sat jogging her babe in her weak arms, and appeasing the other children by saying that brother had gone to their uncle for food, and soon the pot would be boiling and they would all be satisfied. When, hearing a foot-fall, all scrambled eagerly to the door, only to see the empty-handed, red-eyed boy coming along, trying manfully to look cheerful.

"Did your uncle whip you?" asked the mother, more eager for the safety of her son, than to have her own crying want allayed.

"No," stammered the brave boy. "He had gone to the capital on business," said he, hoping to thus prevent further questioning, on so troublesome a subject.

"What shall I do"? queried the poor woman, amidst the crying and moaning of her children. There was nothing to do but starve, it seemed. However, she thought of her own straw shoes, which were scarcely used, and these she sent to the market, where they brought three *cash* (3/15 of a cent). This pittance was invested equally in rice, beans, and vegetables; eating which they were relieved for the present, and with full stomachs the little ones fell to playing happily once more, but the poor mother was full of anxiety for the morrow.

Their fortune had turned, however, with their new lease of life, for the father returned with a bale of faggots he had gathered on the mountains, and with the proceeds of these the shoes were redeemed and more food was purchased. Bright and early then next morning both parents went forth in search of work. The wife secured employment winnowing rice. The husband overtook a boy bearing a pack, but his back was so blistered, he could with difficulty carry his burden. Hyung Bo adjusted the saddle of the pack frame to his own back, and carried it for the boy, who, at their arrival at his destination in the evening, gave his helper some cash, in addition to his lodging and meals. During the night, however, a gentleman wished to send a letter by rapid dispatch to a distant place, and Hyung Bo was paid well for carrying it.

Returning from this profitable errand, he heard of a very rich man, who had been seized by the corrupt local magistrate, on a false accusation, and was to be beaten publicly, unless he consented to pay a heavy sum as hush money. Hearing of this, Hyung went to see the rich prisoner, and arranged with him that he would act as his substitute for three thousand cash (two dollars). The man was very glad to get off so easily, and Hyung took the beating. He limped to his house, where his poor wife greeted him with tears and lamentations, for he was a sore and sorry sight indeed. He was cheerful, however, for he explained to them that this had been a rich day's work; he had simply submitted to a little whipping, and was to get three thousand cash for it.

The money did not come, however, for the fraud was detected, and the original prisoner was also punished. Being of rather a close disposition, the man seemed to think it unnecessary to pay for what did him no good. Then the wife cried indeed over her husband's wrongs and their own more unfortunate condition. But the husband cheered her, saying: "If we do right we will surely succeed." He was right. Spring was coming on, and he soon got work at plowing and sowing seed. They gave their little house the usual spring cleaning, and decorated the door with appropriate legends, calling upon the fates to bless with prosperity the little home.

With the spring came the birds from the south country, and they seemed to have a preference for the home of this poor family—as indeed did the rats and insects. The birds built their nests under the eaves. They were swallows, and as they made their little mud air-castles, Hyung Bo said to his wife: "I am afraid to have these birds build their nests there. Our house is so weak it may fall down, and then what will the poor birds do?" But the little visitors seemed not alarmed, and remained with the kind people, apparently feeling safe under the friendly roof.

By and by the little nests were full of commotion and bluster; the eggs had opened, and circles of wide opened mouths could be seen in every nest. Hyung and his children were greatly interested in this new addition to their family circle, and often gave them bits of their own scanty allowance of food, so that the birds became quite tame and hopped in and out of the hut at will.

One day, when the little birds were taking their first lesson in flying, Hyung was lying on his back on the ground, and saw a huge roof-snake crawl along and devour several little birds before he could arise and help them. One bird struggled from the reptile and fell, but, catching both legs in the fine meshes of a reed-blind, they were broken, and the little fellow hung helplessly within the snake's reach. Hyung hastily snatched it down, and with the help of his wife he bound up the broken limbs, using dried fish-skin for splints. He laid the little patient in a warm place, and the bones speedily united, so that the bird soon began to hop around the room, and pick up bits of food laid out for him. Soon the splints were removed, however, and he flew away, happily, to join his fellows.

The autumn came; and one evening—it was the ninth day of the ninth moon—as the little family were sitting about the door, they noticed the bird with the crooked legs sitting on the clothes-line and singing to them.

"I believe he is thanking us and saying good-by," said Hyung, "for the birds are all going south now."

That seemed to be the truth, for they saw their little friend no longer, and they felt lonely without the occupants of the now deserted nests. The birds, however, were paying homage to the king of birds in the bird-land beyond the frosts. And as the king saw the little crooked-legged bird come along, he demanded an explanation of the strange sight. Thereupon the little fellow related his narrow escape from a snake that had already devoured many of his brothers and cousins, the accident in the blind, and his rescue and subsequent treatment by a very poor but very kind man.

His bird majesty was very much entertained and pleased. He thereupon gave the little cripple a seed engraved with fine characters in gold, denoting that the seed belonged to the gourd family. This seed the bird was to give to his benefactor in the spring.

The winter wore away, and the spring found the little family almost as destitute as when first we described them. One day they heard a familiar bird song, and, running out, they saw their little crooked-legged friend with something in its mouth, that looked like a seed. Dropping its burden to the ground, the little bird sang to them of the king's gratitude, and of the present he had sent, and then flew away.

Hyung picked up the seed with curiosity, and on one side he saw the name of its kind, on the other, in fine gold characters, was a message saying: "Bury me in soft earth, and give me plenty of water." They did so, and in four days the little shoot appeared in the fine earth. They watched its remarkable growth with eager interest as the stem shot up, and climbed all over the house, covering it up as a bower, and threatening to break down the frail structure with the added weight. It blossomed, and soon four small gourds began to form. They grew to an enormous size, and Hyung could scarcely keep from cutting them. His wife prevailed on him to wait till the frost had made them ripe, however, as then they could cut them, eat the inside, and make water-vessels of the shells, which they could then sell, and thus make a double profit. He waited, though with a poor grace, till the ninth moon, when the gourds were left alone, high upon the roof, with only a trace of the shrivelled stems which had planted them there.

Hyung got a saw and sawed open the first huge gourd. He worked so long, that when his task was finished he feared he must be in a swoon, for out of the opened gourd stepped two beautiful boys, with fine bottles of wine and a table of jade set with dainty cups. Hyung staggered back and sought assurance of his wife, who was fully as dazed as was her husband. The surprise was somewhat relieved by one of the handsome youths stepping forth, placing the table before them, and announcing that the bird king had sent them with these presents to the benefactor of one of his subjects—the bird with broken legs. Ere they could answer, the other youth placed a silver bottle on the table, saying: "This wine will restore life to the dead." Another, which he placed on the table, would, he said, restore sight to the blind. Then going to the gourd, he brought two gold bottles, one contained a tobacco, which, being smoked, would give speech to the dumb, while the other gold bottle contained wine, which would prevent the approach of age and ward off death.

Having made these announcements, the pair disappeared, leaving Hyung and his wife almost dumb with amazement. They looked at the gourd, then at the little table and its contents, and each looked at the other to be sure it was not a dream. At length Hyung broke the silence, remarking that, as he was very hungry, he would venture to open another gourd, in the hope that it would be found full of something good to eat, since it was not so important for him to have something with which to restore life just now as it was to have something to sustain life with.

The next gourd was opened as was the first, when by some means out flowed all manner of household furniture, and clothing, with rolls upon rolls of fine silk and satin cloth, linen goods, and the finest cotton. The satin alone was far greater in bulk than the gourd had been, yet, in addition, the premises were literally strewn with costly furniture and the finest fabrics. They barely examined the goods now, their amazement having become so great that they could scarcely wait until all had been opened, and the whole seemed so unreal, that they feared delay might be dangerous. Both sawed away on the next gourd, when out came a body of carpenters, all equipped with tools and lumber, and, to their utter and complete amazement, began putting up a house as quickly and quietly as thought, so that before they could arise from the ground they saw a fine house standing before them, with courts and servants' quarters, stables, and granaries. Simultaneously a great train of bulls and ponies appeared, loaded down with rice and other products as tributes from the district in which the place was located. Others came bringing money tribute, servants, male and female, and clothing.

They felt sure they were in dreamland now, and that they might enjoy the exercise of power while it lasted, they began commanding the servants to put the goods away, the money in the *sahrang*, or reception-room, the clothing in the *tarack*, or garret over the fireplace, the rice in the granaries, and animals in their stables. Others were sent to prepare a bath, that they might don the fine clothing before it should be too late. The servants obeyed, increasing the astonishment of the pair, and causing them to literally forget the fourth gourd in their amazed contemplation of the wondrous miracles being performed, and the dreamy air of satisfaction and contentment with which it surrounded them.

Their attention was called to the gourd by the servants, who were then commanded to carefully saw it open. They did so, and out stepped a maiden, as beautiful as were the gifts that had preceded her. Never before had Hyung looked on any one who could at all compare with the matchless beauty and grace of the lovely creature who now stood so modestly and confidingly before him. He could find no words to express his boundless admiration, and could only stand in mute wonder and feast himself upon her beauty. Not so with his wife, however. She saw only a rival in the beautiful girl, and straightway demanded who she was, whence she came, and what she wanted. The maid replied: "I am sent by the bird king to be this man's concubine." Whereupon the wife grew dark in the face, and ordered her to go whence she came and not see her husband again. She upbraided him for not being content with a house and estate, numbers of retainers and quantities of money, and declared this last trouble was all due to his greed in opening the fourth gourd.

Her husband had by this time found his speech, however, and severely reprimanding her for conducting herself in such a manner upon the receipt of such heavenly gifts, while yesterday she had been little more than a beggar; he commanded her to go at once to the women's quarters, where she should reign supreme, and never make such a display of her ill-temper again, under penalty of being consigned to a house by herself. The maiden he gladly welcomed, and conducted her to apartments set aside for her.

II.

When Nahl Bo heard of the wonderful change taking place at his brother's establishment, he went himself to look into the matter. He found the report not exaggerated, and began to upbraid his brother with dishonest methods, which accusation the brother stoutly denied, and further demanded where, and of whom, he could steal a house, such rich garments, fine furniture, and have it removed in a day to the site of his former hovel. Nahl Bo demanded an explanation, and Hyung Bo frankly told him how he had saved the bird from the snake and had bound up its broken limbs, so that it recovered; how the bird in return brought him a seed engraved with gold characters, instructing him how to plant and rear it; and how, having done so, the four gourds were born on the stalk, and from them, on ripening, had appeared these rich gifts. The ill-favored brother even then persisted in his charges, and in a gruff, ugly manner accused Hyung Bo of being worse than a thief in keeping all these fine goods, instead of dutifully sharing them with his elder brother. This insinuation of undutiful conduct really annoyed Hyung Bo, who, in his kindness of heart, forgave this unbrotherly senior, his former ill conduct, and thinking only of his own present good fortune, he kindly bestowed considerable gifts upon the undeserving brother, and doubtless would have done more but that the covetous man espyed the fair maiden, and at once insisted on having her. This was too much even for the patient Hyung Bo, who refused with a determination remarkable for him. A quarrel ensued, during which the elder brother took his departure in a rage, fully determined to use the secret of his brother's success for all it was worth in securing rich gifts for himself.

Going home he struck at all the birds he could see, and ordered his servants to do the same. After killing many, he succeeded in catching one, and, breaking its legs, he took fish-skin and bound them up in splints, laying the little sufferer in a warm place, till it recovered and flew away, bandages and all. The result was as expected. The bird being questioned by the bird king concerning its crooked legs, related its story, dwelling, however, on the man's cruelty in killing so many birds and then breaking its own legs. The king understood thoroughly, and gave the little cripple a seed to present to the wicked man on its return in the spring.

Springtime came, and one day, as Nahl Bo was sitting cross-legged in the little room opening on the veranda off his court, he heard a familiar bird-song. Dropping his long pipe, he threw open the paper windows, and there, sure enough, sat a crooked-legged bird on the clothes line, bearing a seed in its mouth. Nahl Bo would let no one touch it, but as the bird dropped the seed and flew away, he jumped out so eagerly that he forgot to slip his shoes on, and got his clean white stockings all befouled. He secured the seed, however, and felt that his fortune was made. He planted it carefully, as directed, and gave it his personal attention.

The vines were most luxurious. They grew with great rapidity, till they had well nigh covered the whole of his large house and out-buildings. Instead of one gourd, or even four, as in the brother's case, the new vines bore twelve gourds, which grew and grew till the great beams of his house fairly groaned under their weight, and he had to block them in place to keep them from rolling off the roofs. He had to hire men to guard them carefully, for now that the source of Hyung Bo's riches was understood, every one was anxious for a gourd. They did not know the secret, however, which Nahl Bo concealed through selfishness, and Hyung through fear that every one would take to killing and maiming birds as his wicked brother had done.

Maintaining a guard was expensive, and the plant so loosened the roof tiles, by the tendrils searching for earth and moisture in the great layer of clay under the tiles, that the rainy season made great havoc with his house. Large portions of plaster from the inside fell upon the paper ceilings, which in turn gave way, letting the dirty water drip into the rooms, and making the house almost uninhabitable. At last, however, the plants could do no more harm; the frost had come, the vines had shrivelled away, and the enormous ripe gourds were carefully lowered, amid the yelling of a score of coolies, as each seemed to get in the others' way trying to manipulate the ropes and poles with which the gourds were let down to the ground. Once inside the court, and the great doors locked, Nahl Bo felt relieved, and shutting out every one but a carpenter and his assistant, he prepared for the great surprise which he knew must await him, in spite of his most vivid dreams.

The carpenter insisted upon the enormous sum of 1,000 cash for opening each gourd, and as he was too impatient to await the arrival of another, and as he expected to be of princely wealth in a few moments, Nahl Bo agreed to the exorbitant price. Whereupon, carefully bracing a gourd, the men began sawing it through. It seemed a long time before the gourd fell in halves. When it did, out came a party of rope-dancers, such as perform at fairs and public places. Nahl Bo was unprepared for any such surprise as this, and fancied it must be some great mistake. They sang and danced about as well as the crowded condition of the court would allow, and the family looked on complacently, supposing that the band had been sent to celebrate their coming good fortune. But Nahl Bo soon had enough of this. He wanted to get at his riches, and seeing that the actors were about to stretch their ropes for a more extensive performance, he ordered them to cease and take their departure. To his amazement, however, they refused to do this, until he had paid them 5,000 cash for their trouble. "You sent for us and we came," said the leader. "Now pay us, or we will live with you till you do." There was no help for it, and with great reluctance and some foreboding, he gave them the money and dismissed them. Then Nahl Bo turned to the carpenter, who chanced to be a man with an ugly visage, made uglier by a great hare-lip. "You," he said, "are the cause of all this. Before you entered this court these gourds were filled with gold, and your ugly face has changed it to beggars."

Number two was opened with no better results, for out came a body of Buddhist priests, begging for their temple, and promising many sons in return for offerings of suitable merit. Although disgusted beyond measure, Nahl Bo still had faith in the gourds, and to get rid of the priests, lest they should see his riches, he gave them also 5,000 cash.

As soon as the priests were gone, gourd number three was opened, with still poorer results, for out came a procession of paid mourners followed by a corpse borne by bearers. The mourners wept as loudly as possible, and all was in a perfect uproar. When ordered to go, the mourners declared they must have money for mourning, and to pay for burying the body. Seeing no possible help for it, 5,000 cash was finally given them, and they went out with the bier. Then Nahl Bo's wife came into the court, and began to abuse the hare-lipped man for bringing upon them all this trouble. Whereupon the latter became angry and demanded his money that he might leave. They had no intention of giving up the search as yet, however, and, as it was too late to change carpenters, the ugly fellow was paid for the work already done, and given an advance on that yet remaining. He therefore set to work upon the fourth gourd, which Nahl Bo watched with feverish anxiety.

From this one there came a band of *gee sang*, or dancing girls. There was one woman from each province, and each had her song and dance. One sang of the *yang wang*, or wind god; another of the *wang jay*, or pan deity; one sang of the *sung jee*, or money that is placed as a christening on the roof tree of every house. There was the cuckoo song. The song of the ancient tree that has lived so long that its heart is dead and gone, leaving but a hollow space, yet the leaves spring forth every spring-tide. The song of laughter and mourning, with an injunction to see to it that the rice offering be made to the departed spirits. To the king of the sun and stars a song was sung. And last of all, one votary sang of the twelve months that make the year, the twelve hours that make the day, the thirty days that make the month, and of the new year's birth, as the old year dies, taking with it their ills to be buried in the past, and reminding all people to celebrate the New Year holidays by donning clean clothes and feasting on good food, that the following year may be to them one of plenty and prosperity. Having finished their songs and their graceful posturing and waving of their gay silk banners, the *gee sang* demanded their pay, which had to be given them, reducing the family wealth 5,000 cash more.

The wife now tried to persuade Nahl Bo to stop and not open more, but the hare-lip man offered to open the next for 500 cash, as he was secretly enjoying the sport. So the fifth was opened a little, when a yellow-looking substance was seen inside, which was taken to be gold, and they hurriedly opened it completely. But instead of gold, out came an acrobatic pair,—being a strong man with a youth dressed to represent a girl. The man danced about, holding his young companion balanced upon his shoulders, singing meanwhile a song of an ancient king, whose riotous living was so distasteful to his subjects that he built him a cavernous palace, the floor of which was covered with quicksilver, the walls were decorated with jewels, and myriad lamps turned the darkness into day. Here were to be found the choicest viands and wines, with bands of music to entertain the feasters: most beautiful women; and he enjoyed himself most luxuriously until his enemy, learning the secret, threw open the cavern to the light of day, when all of the beautiful women immediately disappeared in the sun's rays.

Before he could get these people to discontinue their performance, Nahl Bo had to give them also 5,000 cash. Yet in spite of all his ill luck, he decided to open another. Which being done, a jester came forth, demanding the expense money for his long journey. This was finally given him, for Nahl Bo had hit upon what he deemed a clever expedient. He took the wise fool aside, and asked him to use his wisdom in pointing out to him which of these gourds contained gold. Whereupon the jester looked wise, tapped several gourds, and motioned to each one as being filled with gold.

The seventh was therefore opened, and a lot of yamen runners came forth, followed by an official. Nahl Bo tried to run from what he knew must mean an exorbitant "squeeze," but he was caught and beaten for his indiscretion. The official called for his valise, and took from it a paper, which his secretary read, announcing that Nahl Bo was the serf of this lord and must hereafter pay to him a heavy tribute. At this they groaned in their hearts, and the wife declared that even now the money was all gone, even to the last cash, while the rabble which had collected had stolen nearly every thing worth removing. Yet the officer's servants demanded pay for their services, and they had to be given a note secured on the property before they would leave. Matters were now so serious that they could not be made much worse, and it was decided to open each remaining gourd, that if there were any gold they might have it.

When the next one was opened a bevy of *moo tang* women (soothsayers) came forth, offering to drive away the spirit of disease and restore the sick to health. They arranged their banners for their usual dancing ceremony, brought forth their drums, with which to exorcise the demons, and called for rice to offer to the spirits and clothes to burn for the spirits' apparel.

"Get out!" roared Nahl Bo. "I am not sick except for the visitation of such as yourselves, who are forever burdening the poor, and demanding pay for your supposed services. Away with you, and befool some other *pah sak ye* (eight month's man—fool) if you can. I want none of your services."

They were no easier to drive away, however, than were the other annoying visitors that had come with his supposed good fortune. He had finally to pay them as he had the others; and dejectedly he sat, scarcely noticing the opening of the ninth gourd.

The latter proved to contain a juggler, and the exasperated Nahl Bo, seeing but one small man, determined to make short work of him. Seizing him by his topknot of hair, he was about to drag him to the door, when the dexterous fellow, catching his tormentor by the thighs, threw him headlong over his own back, nearly breaking his neck, and causing him to lie stunned for a time, while the expert bound him hand and foot, and stood him on his head, so that the wife was glad to pay the fellow and dismiss him ere the life should be departed from her lord.

On opening the tenth a party of blind men came out, picking their way with their long sticks, while their sightless orbs were raised towards the unseen heavens. They offered to tell the fortunes of the family. But, while their services might have been demanded earlier, the case was now too desperate for any such help. The old men tinkled their little bells, and chanted some poetry addressed to the four good spirits stationed at the four corners of the earth, where they patiently stand bearing the world upon their shoulders; and to the distant heavens that arch over and fold the earth in their embrace, where the two meet at the far horizon (as pictured in the Korean flag). The blind men threw their dice, and, fearing lest they should prophesy death, Nahl Bo quickly paid and dismissed them.

The next gourd was opened but a trifle, that they might first determine as to the wisdom of letting out its contents. Before they could determine, however, a voice like thunder was heard from within, and the huge form of a giant arose, splitting open the gourd as he came forth. In his anger he seized poor Nahl Bo and tossed him upon his shoulders as though he would carry him away. Whereupon the wife plead with tears for his release, and gladly gave an order for the amount of the ransom. After which the monster allowed the frightened man to fall to the ground, nearly breaking his aching bones in the fall.

The carpenter did not relish the sport any longer; it seemed to be getting entirely too dangerous. He thereupon demanded the balance of his pay, which they finally agreed to give him, providing he would open the last remaining gourd. For the desperate people hoped to find this at least in sufficient condition that they might cook or make soup of it, since they had no food left at all and no money, while the other gourds were so spoiled by the tramping of the feet of their unbidden guests, as to be totally unfit for food.

The man did as requested, but had only sawed a very little when the gourd split open as though it were rotten, while a most awful stench arose, driving every one from the premises. This was followed by a gale of wind, so severe as to destroy the buildings, which, in falling, took fire from the *kang,* and while the once prosperous man looked on in helpless misery, the last of his remaining property was swept forever from him.

The seed that had brought prosperity to his honest, deserving brother had turned prosperity into ruin to the cruel, covetous Nahl Bo, who now had to subsist upon the charity of his kind brother, whom he had formerly treated so cruelly.

CHUN YANG THE FAITHFUL DANCING-GIRL WIFE

In the city of Nam Won, in Chull Lah Do (the southern province of Korea), lived the Prefect Ye Tung Uhi. He was the happy father of a son of some sixteen years of age. Being an only child the boy was naturally much petted. He was not an ordinary young man, however, for in addition to a handsome, manly face and stalwart figure, he possessed a bright, quick mind, and was naturally clever. A more dutiful son could not be found. He occupied a house in the rear of his father's quarters, and devoted himself to his books, going regularly each evening to make his obeisance to his father, and express his wish that pleasant, refreshing sleep might come to him; then, in the morning, before breakfasting, he was wont to go and enquire how the new day had found his father.

The Prefect was but recently appointed to rule over the Nam Won district when the events about to be recorded occurred. The winter months had been spent mostly indoors, but as the mild spring weather approached and the buds began to open to the singing of the joyful birds, Ye Toh Ryung, or Toh Ryung, the son, felt that he must get out and enjoy nature. Like an animal that has buried itself in a hole in the earth, he came forth rejoicing; the bright yellow birds welcomed him from the willow trees, the soft breezes fanned his cheeks, and the freshness of the air exhilarated him. He called his *pang san* (valet) and asked him concerning the neighboring views. The servant was a native of the district, and knew the place well; he enumerated the various places especially prized for their scenery, but concluded with: "But of all rare views, 'Kang Hal Loo' is the rarest.

Officers from the eight provinces come to enjoy the scenery, and the temple is covered with verses they have left in praise of the place." "Very well, then, we will go there," said Toh Ryung "Go you and clean up the place for my reception."

The servant hurried off to order the temple swept and spread with clean mats, while his young master sauntered along almost intoxicated by the freshness and new life of every thing around him. Arrived at the place, after a long, tedious ascent of the mountain side, he flung himself upon a huge bolster-like cushion, and with half-closed eyes, drank in the beauty of the scene along with the balmy, perfume-laden spring zephyrs. He called his servant, and congratulated him upon his taste, declaring that were the gods in search of a fine view, they could not find a place that would surpass this; to which the man answered:

"That is true; so true, in fact, that it is well known that the spirits do frequent this place for its beauty."

As he said this, Toh Ryung had raised himself, and was leaning on one arm, gazing out toward one side, when, as though it were one of the spirits just mentioned, the vision of a beautiful girl shot up into the air and soon fell back out of sight in the shrubbery of an adjoining court-yard. He could just get a confused picture of an angelic face, surrounded by hair like the black thunder-cloud, a neck of ravishing beauty, and a dazzle of bright silks,—when the whole had vanished. He was dumb with amazement, for he felt sure he must have seen one of the spirits said to frequent the place; but before he could speak, the vision arose again, and he then had time to see that it was but a beautiful girl swinging in her dooryard. He did not move, he scarcely breathed, but sat with bulging eyes absorbing the prettiest view he had ever seen. He noted the handsome, laughing face, the silken black hair, held back in a coil by a huge coral pin; he saw the jewels sparkling on the gay robes, the dainty white hands and full round arms, from which the breezes blew back the sleeves; and as she flew higher in her wild sport, oh, joy! two little shoeless feet encased in white stockings, shot up among the peach blossoms, causing them to fall in showers all about her. In the midst of the sport her hairpin loosened and fell, allowing her raven locks to float about her shoulders; but, alas! the costly ornament fell on a rock and broke, for Toh Ryung could hear the sharp click where he sat. This ended the sport, and the little maid disappeared, all unconscious of the agitation she had caused in a young man's breast by her harmless spring exercise.

After some silence, the young man asked his servant if he had seen any thing, for even yet he feared his mind had been wandering close to the dreamland. After some joking, the servant confessed to having seen the girl swinging, whereupon his master demanded her name. "She is Uhl Mahs' daughter, a *gee sang* (public dancing girl) of this city; her name is Chun Yang Ye"—fragrant spring. "*I yah!* superb; I can see her then, and have her sing and dance for me," exclaimed Toh Ryung. "Go and call her at once, you slave."

The man ran, over good road and bad alike, up hill and down, panting as he went; for while the back of the women's quarters of the adjoining compound was near at hand, the entrance had to be reached by a long circuit. Arriving out of breath, he pounded at the gate, calling the girl by name.

"Who is that calls me?" she enquired when the noise had attracted her attention.

"Oh, never mind who," answered the exhausted man, "it is great business; open the door."

"Who are you, and what do you want?"

"I am nobody, and I want nothing; but Ye Toh Ryung is the Governor's son, and he wants to see the Fragrant Spring."

"Who told Ye Toh Ryung my name?"

"Never mind who told him; if you did not want him to know you, then why did you swing so publicly? The great man's son came here to rest and see the beautiful views; he saw you swinging, and can see nothing since. You must go, but you need not fear. He is a gentleman, and will treat you nicely; if your dancing pleases him as did your swinging, he may present you with rich gifts, for he is his father's only son."

Regretting in her proud spirit that fates had placed her in a profession where she was expected to entertain the nobility whether it suited her or not, the girl combed and arranged her hair, tightened her sash, smoothed her disordered clothes, and prepared to look as any vain woman would wish who was about to be presented to the handsomest and most gifted young nobleman of the province. She followed the servant slowly till they reached Toh Ryung's stopping place. She waited while the servant announced her arrival, for a gee sang must not enter a nobleman's presence unbidden. Toh Ryung was too excited to invite her in, however, and his servant had to prompt him, when, laughing at his own agitation, he pleasantly bade her enter and sit down.

"What is your name?" asked he.

"My name is Chun Yang Ye," she said, with a voice that resembled silver jingling in a pouch.

"How old are you?"

"My age is just twice eight years."

"Ah ha!" laughed the now composed boy, "how fortunate; you are twice eight, and I am four fours. We are of the same age. Your name, Fragrant Spring, is the same as your face—very beautiful. Your cheeks are like the petals of the *mah hah* that ushers in the soft spring. Your eyes are like those of the eagle sitting on the ancient tree, but soft and gentle as the moonlight," ran on the enraptured youth. "When is your birthday?"

"My birthday occurs at midnight on the eighth day of the fourth moon," modestly replied the flattered girl, who was quickly succumbing to the charms of the ardent and handsome young fellow, whose heart she could see was already her own.

"Is it possible?" exclaimed he; "that is the date of the lantern festival, and it is also my own birthday, only I was born at eleven instead of twelve. I am sorry I was not born at twelve now. But it doesn't matter. Surely the gods had some motive in sending us into the world at the same time, and thus bringing us together at our sixteenth spring-tide. Heaven must have intended us to be man and wife"; and he bade her sit still as she started as though to take her departure. Then he began to plead with her, pacing the room in his excitement, till his attendant likened the sound to the combat of ancient warriors. "This chance meeting of ours has a meaning," he argued. "Often when the buds were bursting, or when the forest trees were turning to fire and blood, have I played and supped with pretty gee sang, watched them dance, and wrote them verses, but never before have I lost my heart; never before have I seen any one so incomparably beautiful. You are no common mortal. You were destined to be my wife; you must be mine, you must marry me."

She wrinkled her fair brow and thought, for she was no silly, foolish thing, and while her heart was almost, if not quite won by this tempestuous lover, yet she saw where his blind love would not let him see. "You know," she said, "the son of a nobleman may not marry a gee sang without the consent of his parents. I know I am a gee sang by name, the fates have so ordained, but, nevertheless, I am an honorable woman, always have been, and expect to remain so."

"Certainly," he answered, "we cannot celebrate the 'six customs ceremony' (parental arrangements, exchange of letters, contracts, exchange of presents, preliminary visits, ceremony proper), but we can be privately married just the same."

"No, it cannot be. Your father would not consent, and should we be privately married, and your father be ordered to duty at some other place, you would not dare take me with you. Then you would marry the daughter of some nobleman, and I would be forgotten. It must not, cannot be," and she arose to depart. "Stay, stay," he begged. "You do me an injustice. I will never forsake you, or marry another. I swear it. And a *yang ban* (noble) has but one mouth, he cannot speak two ways. Even should we leave this place I will take you with me, or return soon to you. You must not refuse me."

"But suppose you change your mind or forget your promises; words fly out of the mouth and are soon lost, ink and paper are more lasting; give me your promises in writing," she says.

Instantly the young man took up paper and brush; having rubbed the ink well, he wrote: "A memorandum. Desiring to enjoy the spring scenery, I came to Kang Hal Loo. There I saw for the first time my heaven-sent bride. Meeting for the first time, I pledge myself for one hundred years; to be her faithful husband. Should I change, show this paper to the magistrate." Folding up the manuscript with care he handed it to her. While putting it into her pocket she said: "Speech has no legs, yet it can travel many thousands of miles. Suppose this matter should reach your father's ears, what would you do?"

"Never fear; my father was once young, who knows but I may be following the example of his early days. I have contracted with you, and we now are married, even my father cannot change it. Should he discover our alliance and disown me, I will still be yours, and together we shall live and die."

She arose to go, and pointing with her jade-like hand to a clump of bamboos, said: "There is my house; as I cannot come to you, you must come to me and make my mother's house your home, as much as your duty to your parents will allow."

As the sun began to burn red above the mountains' peaks, they bade each other a fond adieu, and each departed for home accompanied by their respective attendants.

Ye Toh Ryung went to his room, which now seemed a prison-like place instead of the pleasant study he had found it. He took up a book, but reading was no satisfaction, every word seemed to transform itself into Chun or Yang. Every thought was of the little maid of the spring fragrance. He changed his books, but it was no use, he could not even keep them right side up, not to mention using them properly. Instead of singing off his lessons as usual, he kept singing, *Chun Yang Ye poh go sip so* (I want to see the spring fragrance), till his father, hearing the confused sounds, sent to ascertain what was the matter with his son. The boy was singing, "As the parched earth cries for rain after the seven years' drought, so my heart pants for my Chun Yang Ye, whose face to me is like the rays of the sun upon the earth after a nine years' rain." He paid no heed to the servants, and soon his father sent his private secretary, demanding what it was the boy desired so much that he should keep singing. "I want to see, I want to see." Toh Ryung answered that he was reading an uninteresting book, and looking for another. Though he remained more quiet after this, he still was all impatience to be off to his sweetheart-wife, and calling his attendant, he sent him out to see how near the sun was to setting. Enjoying the sport, the man returned, saying the sun was now high over head.

"Begone," said he, "can any one hold back the sun; it had reached the mountain tops before I came home."

At last the servant brought his dinner, for which he had no appetite. He could ill abide the long delay between the dinner hour and the regular time for his father's retiring. The time did come, however, and when the lights were extinguished and his father had gone to sleep, he took his trusty servant, and, scaling the back wall, they hurried to the house of Chun Yang Ye.

As they approached they heard someone playing the harp, and singing of the "dull pace of the hours when one's lover is away." Being admitted, they met the mother, who, with some distrust, received Toh Ryung's assurances and sent him to her daughter's apartments.

The house pleased him; it was neat and well-appointed. The public room, facing the court, was lighted by a blue lantern, which in the mellow light resembled a pleasure barge drifting on the spring flood. Banners of poetry hung upon the walls. Upon the door leading to Chun Yang's little parlor hung a banner inscribed with verses to her ancestors and descendants, praying that "a century be short to span her life and happiness, and that her children's children be blessed with prosperity for a thousand years." Through the open windows could be seen moonlight glimpses of the little garden of the swinging girl. There was a miniature lake almost filled with lotus plants, where two sleepy swans floated with heads beneath their wings, while the occasional gleam of a gold or silver scale showed that the water was inhabited. A summer-house on the water's edge was almost covered with fragrant spring blossoms, the whole being enclosed in a little grove of bamboo and willows, that shut out the view of outsiders.

While gazing at this restful sight, Chun Yang Ye herself came out, and all was lost in the lustre of her greater beauty. She asked him into her little parlor, where was a profusion of choice carved cabinets and ornaments of jade and metal, while richly embroidered mats covered the highly-polished floor. She was so delighted that she took both his hands in her pretty, white, soft ones, and gazing longingly into each other's eyes, she led him into another room, where, on a low table, a most elegant lunch was spread. They sat down on the floor and surveyed the loaded table. There were fruits preserved in sugar, candied nuts arranged in many dainty, nested boxes; sweet pickles and confections, pears that had grown in the warmth of a summer now dead, and grapes that had been saved from decay by the same sun that had called them forth. Quaint old bottles with long, twisted necks, contained choice medicated wines, to be drunk from the little crackled cups, such as the ancients used.

Pouring out a cup, she sang to him: "This is the elixir of youth; drinking this, may you never grow old; though ten thousand years pass over your head, may you stand like the mountain that never changes." He drank half of the cup's contents, and praised her sweet voice, asking for another song. She sang: "Let us drain the cup while we may. In the grave who will be our cup-bearer. While we are young let us play. When old, mirth gives place to care. The flowers can bloom but a few days at best, and must then die, that the seed may be born. The moon is no sooner full than it begins to wane, that the young moon may rise."

The sentiments suited him, the wine exhilarated him, and his spirits rose. He drained his cup, and called for more wine and song; but she restrained him. They ate the dainty food, and more wine and song followed. She talked of the sweet contract they had made, and anon they pledged themselves anew. Not content with promises for this short life, they went into the future, and he yielded readily to her request, that when death should at last o'ertake them, she would enter a flower, while he would become a butterfly, coming and resting on her bosom, and feasting off her fragrant sweetness.

The father did not know of his son's recent alliance, though the young man honestly went and removed Chun Yang's name from the list of the district gee sang, kept in his father's office; for, now that she was a married woman, she need no longer go out with the dancing-girls. Every morning, as before, the dutiful son presented himself before his father, with respectful inquiries after his health, and his rest the preceding night. But, nevertheless, each night the young man's apartments were deserted, while he spent the time in the house of his wife.

Thus the months rolled on with amazing speed. The lovers were in paradise. The father enjoyed his work, and labored hard for the betterment of the condition of his subjects. Never before had so large a tribute been sent by this district. Yet the people were not burdened as much as when far less of their products reached the government granaries. The honest integrity of the officer reached the King in many reports, and when a vacancy occurred at the head of the Treasury Department, he was raised to be Ho Joh Pansa (Secretary of Finance). Delighted, the father sent for his son and told him the news, but, to his amazement, the young man had naught to say, in fact he seemed as one struck dumb, as well he might. Within himself there was a great tumult; his heart beat so violently as to seem perceptible, and at times it arose and filled his throat, cutting off any speech he might wish to utter. Surprised at the conduct of his son, the father bade him go and inform his mother, that she might order the packing to commence.

He went; but soon found a chance to fly to Chun Yang, who, at first, was much concerned for his health, as his looks denoted a serious illness. When he had made her understand, however, despair seized her, and they gazed at each other in mute dismay and utter helplessness. At last she seemed to awaken from her stupor, and, in an agony of despair, she beat her breast, and moaned: "Oh, how can we separate. We must die, we cannot live apart"; and tears coming to her relief, she cried: "If we say good-by, it will be forever; we can never meet again. Oh, I feared it; we have been too happy—too happy. The one who made this order is a murderer; it must be my death. If you go to Seoul and leave me, I must die. I am but a poor weak woman, and I cannot live without you."

He took her, and laying her head on his breast, tried to soothe her. "Don't cry so bitterly," he begged; "my heart is almost broken now. I cannot bear it. I wish it could always be spring-time; but this is only like the cruel winter that, lingering in the mountain, sometimes sweeps down the valley, drives out the spring, and kills the blossoms. We will not give up and die, though. We have contracted for one hundred years, and this will be but a bitter separation that will make our speedy reunion more blissful."

"Oh," she says, "but how can I live here alone, with you in Seoul? Just think of the long, tedious summer days, the long and lonely winter nights. I must see no one. I cannot know of you, for who will tell me, and how am I to endure it?"

"Had not my father been given this great honor, we would perhaps not have been parted; as it is I must go, there is no help for it, but you must believe me when I promise I will come again. Here, take this crystal mirror as a pledge that I will keep my word"; and he gave her his pocket-mirror of rock crystal.

"Promise me when you will return," said she; and then, without awaiting an answer, she sang: "When the sear and withered trunk begins to bloom, and the dead bird sings in the branches, then my lover will come to me. When the river flows over the eastern mountains, then may I see him glide along in his ship to me." He chided her for her lack of faith, and assured her again it was as hard for one as the other. After a time she became more reconciled, and taking off her jade ring, gave it to him for a keepsake, saying: "My love, like this ring, knows no end. You must go, alas! but my love will go with you, and may it protect you when crossing wild mountains and distant rivers, and bring you again safely to me. If you go to Seoul, you must not trifle, but take your books, study hard, and enter the examinations, then, perhaps, you may obtain rank and come to me. I will stand with my hand shading my eyes, ever watching for your return."

Promising to cherish her speech, with her image in his breast, they made their final adieu, and tore apart.

The long journey seemed like a funeral to the lover. Everywhere her image rose before him. He could think of nothing else; but by the time he arrived at the capital he had made up his mind as to his future course, and from that day forth his parents wondered at his stern, determined manner. He shut himself up in his room with his books. He would neither go out, or form acquaintances among the young noblemen of the gay city. Thus he spent months in hard study, taking no note of passing events.

In the meantime a new magistrate came to Nam Won. He was a hard-faced, hard-hearted politician. He associated with the dissolute, and devoted himself to riotous living, instead of caring for the welfare of the people. He had not been long in the place till he had heard so much of the matchless beauty of Chun Yang Ye that he determined to see, and if, as reported, marry her. Accordingly he called the clerk of the yamen, and asked concerning "the beautiful gee sang Chun Yang Ye." The clerk answered that such a name had appeared on the records of the dancing girls, but that it had been removed, as she had contracted a marriage with the son of the previous magistrate, and was now a lady of position and respectability.

"You lying rascal!" yelled the enraged officer, who could ill brook any interference with plans he had formed. "A nobleman's son cannot really marry a dancing girl; leave my presence at once, and summon this remarkable 'lady' to appear before me." The clerk could only do as he was bidden, and, summoning the yamen runners, he sent to the house of Chun Yang Ye to acquaint her with the official order.

The runners, being natives of the locality, were loath to do as commanded, and when the fair young woman gave them "wine money" they willingly agreed to report her "too sick to attend the court." Upon doing so, however, the wrath of their master came down upon them. They were well beaten, and then commanded to go with a chair and bring the woman, sick or well, while if they disobeyed him a second time they would be put to death.

Of course they went, but after they had explained to Chun Yang Ye their treatment, her beauty and concern for their safety so affected them, that they offered to go back without her, and face their doom. She would not hear to their being sacrificed for her sake, and prepared to accompany them. She disordered her hair, soiled her fair face, and clad herself in dingy, ill-fitting gowns, which, however, seemed only to cause her natural beauty the more to shine forth. She wept bitterly on entering the yamen, which fired the anger of the official. He ordered her to stop her crying or be beaten, and then as he looked at her disordered and tear-stained face, that resembled choice jade spattered with mud, he found that her beauty was not overstated.

"What does your conduct mean?" said he. "Why have you not presented yourself at this office with the other gee sang?"

"Because, though born a gee sang, I am by marriage a lady, and not subject to the rules of my former profession," she answered.

"Hush!" roared the Prefect. "No more of this nonsense. Present yourself here with the other gee sang, or pay the penalty."

"Never" she bravely cried. "A thousand deaths first. You have no right to exact such a thing of me. You are the King's servant, and should see that the laws are executed, rather than violated."

The man was fairly beside himself with wrath at this, and ordered her chained and thrown into prison at once. The people all wept with her, which but increased her oppressor's anger, and calling the jailer he ordered him to treat her with especial rigor, and be extra vigilant lest some sympathizers should assist her to escape. The jailer promised, but nevertheless he made things as easy for her as was possible under the circumstances. Her mother came and moaned over her daughter's condition, declaring that she was foolish in clinging to her faithless husband, who had brought all this trouble upon them. The neighbors, however, upbraided the old woman for her words, and assured the daughter that she had done just right, and would yet be rewarded. They brought presents of food, and endeavored to make her condition slightly less miserable by their attentions.

She passed the night in bowing before Heaven and calling on the gods and her husband to release her, and in the morning when her mother came, she answered the latter's inquiries as to whether she was alive or not, in a feeble voice which alarmed her parent.

"I am still alive, but surely dying. I can never see my Toh Ryung again; but when I am dead you must take my body to Seoul and bury it near the road over which he travels the most, that even in death I may be near him, though separated in life." Again the mother scolded her for her devotion and for making the contract that binds her strongly to such a man. She could stand it no longer, and begged her mother that she would go away and come to see her no more if she had no pleasanter speech than such to make. "I followed the dictates of my heart and my mind. I did what was right. Can I foretell the future? Because the sun shines to-day are we assured that to-morrow it will shine? The deed is done. I do not regret it; leave me to my grief, but do not add to it by your unkindness."

Thus the days lengthened into months, but she seemed like one dead, and took no thought of time or its flight. She was really ill, and would have died but for the kindness of the jailer. At last one night she dreamed that she was in her own room, dressing, and using the little mirror Toh Ryung had given her, when, without apparent cause, it suddenly broke in halves. She awoke, startled, and felt sure that death was now to liberate her from her sorrows, for what other meaning could the strange occurrence have than that her body was thus to be broken. Although anxious to die and be free, she could not bear the thought of leaving this world without a last look at her loved husband whose hands alone could close her eyes when her spirit had departed. Pondering much upon the dream, she called the jailer and asked him to summon a blind man, as she wished her fortune told. The jailer did so. It was no trouble, for almost as she spoke they heard one picking his way along the street with his long stick, and uttering his peculiar call. He came in and sat down, when they soon discovered that they were friends, for before the man became blind he had been in comfortable circumstances, and had known her father intimately. She therefore asked him to be to her as a kind father, and faithfully tell her when and how death would come to her. He said: "When the blossoms fade and fall they do not die, their life simply enters the seed to bloom again. Death to you would but liberate your spirit to shine again in a fairer body."

She thanked him for his kind generalities, but was impatient, and telling her dream, she begged a careful interpretation of it. He promptly answered, that to be an ill omen a mirror in breaking must make a noise. And on further questioning, he found that in her dream a bird had flown into the room just as the mirror was breaking.

"I see," said he. "The bird was bearer of good news, and the breaking of the mirror, which Toh Ryung gave you, indicates that the news concerned him; let us see." Thereupon he arranged a bunch of sticks, shook them well, while uttering his chant, and threw them upon the floor. Then he soon answered that the news was good. "Your husband has done well. He has passed his examinations, been promoted, and will soon come to you."

She was too happy to believe it, thinking the old man had made it up to please his old friend's distressed child. Yet she cherished the dream and the interpretation in her breast, finding in it solace to her weary, troubled heart.

In the meantime Ye Toh Ryung had continued his studious work day and night, to the anxiety of his parents. Just as he began to feel well prepared for the contest he awaited, a royal proclamation announced, that owing to the fact that peace reigned throughout the whole country, that the closing year had been one of prosperity, and no national calamity had befallen the country, His Gracious Majesty had ordered a grand *guaga*, or competitive examination, to be held. As soon as it became known, literary pilgrims began to pour in from all parts of the country, bent on improving their condition.

The day of the examination found a vast host seated on the grass in front of the pavilion where His Majesty and his officers were. Ye Toh Ryung was given as a subject for his composition, "A lad playing in the shade of a pine tree is questioned by an aged wayfarer."

The young man long rubbed his ink-stick on the stone, thinking very intently meanwhile, but when he began to write in the beautiful characters for which he was noted he seemed inspired, and the composition rolled forth as though he had committed it from the ancient classics. He made the boy express such sentiments of reverence to age as would have charmed the ancients, and the wisdom he put into the conversation was worthy of a king. The matter came so freely that his task was soon finished; in fact many were still wrinkling their brows in preliminary thought, while he was carefully folding up his paper, concealing his name so that the author should not be recognized till the paper had been judged on its merits. He tossed his composition into the pen, and it was at once inspected, being the first one, and remarkably quickly done. When His Majesty heard it read, and saw the perfect characters, he was astonished. Such excellence in writing, composition, and sentiment was unparalleled, and before any other papers were received it was known that none could excel this one. The writer's name was ascertained, and the King was delighted to learn that 'twas the son of his favorite officer. The young man was sent for, and received the congratulations of his King. The latter gave him the usual three glasses of wine, which he drank with modesty. He was then given a wreath of flowers from the King's own hands; the court hat was presented to him, with lateral wings, denoting the rapidity—as the flight of a bird—with which he must execute his Sovereign's commands. Richly embroidered breast-plates were given him, to be worn over the front and back of his court robes. He then went forth, riding on a gayly caparisoned horse, preceded by a band of palace musicians and attendants. Everywhere he was greeted with the cheers of the populace, as for three days he devoted his time to this public display. This duty having been fulfilled, he devotedly went to the graves of his ancestors, and prostrated himself with offerings before them, bemoaning the fact that they could not be present to rejoice in his success. He then presented himself before his King, humbly thanking him for his gracious condescension in bestowing such great honors upon one so utterly unworthy.

His Sovereign was pleased, and told the young man to strive to imitate the example of his honest father. He then asked him what position he wished. Ye Toh Ryung answered that he wished no other position than one that would enable him to be of service to his King. "The year has been one of great prosperity," said he. "The plentiful harvest will tempt corrupt men to oppress the people to their own advantage. I would like, therefore, should it meet with Your Majesty's approval, to undertake the arduous duties of *Ussd*"—government inspector.

He said this as he knew he would then be free to go in search of his wife, while he could also do much good at the same time. The King was delighted, and had his appointment—a private one naturally—made at once, giving him the peculiar seal of the office.

The new Ussa disguised himself as a beggar, putting on straw sandals, a broken hat, underneath which his hair, uncombed and without the encircling band to hold it in place, streamed out in all directions. He wore no white strip in the neck of his shabby gown, and with dirty face he certainly presented a beggarly appearance. Presenting himself at the stables outside of the city, where horses and attendants are provided for the ussas, he soon arranged matters by showing his seal, and with proper attendants started on his journey towards his former home in the southern province.

Arriving at his destination, he remained outside in a miserable hamlet while his servants went into the city to investigate the people and learn the news.

It was spring-time again. The buds were bursting, the birds were singing, and in the warm valley a band of farmers were plowing with lazy bulls, and singing, meanwhile, a grateful song in praise of their just King, their peaceful, prosperous country, and their full stomachs. As the Ussa came along in his disguise he began to jest with them, but they did not like him, and were rude in their jokes at his expense; when an old man, evidently the father, cautioned them to be careful. "Don't you see," said he, "this man's speech is only half made up of our common talk; he is playing a part. I think he must be a gentleman in disguise." The Ussa drew the old man into conversation, asking about various local events, and finally questioning him concerning the character of the Prefect. "Is he just or oppressive, drunken or sober? Does he devote himself to his duties, or give himself up to riotous living?" "Our Magistrate we know little of. His heart is as hard and unbending as the dead heart of the ancient oak. He cares not for the people; the people care not for him but to avoid him. He extorts rice and money unjustly, and spends his ill-gotten gains in riotous living. He has imprisoned and beaten the fair Chun Yang Ye because she repulsed him, and she now lies near to death in the prison, because she married and is true to the poor dog of a son of our former just magistrate."

Ye Toh Ryung was stung by these unjust remarks, filled with the deepest anxiety for his wife, and the bitterest resentment toward the brute of an official, whom, he promised himself, soon to bring to justice. As he moved away, too full of emotion for further conversation, he heard the farmers singing, "Why are some men born to riches, others born to toil, some to marry and live in peace, others too poor to possess a hut."

He walked away meditating. He had placed himself down on the people's level, and began to feel with them. Thus meditating he crossed a valley, through which a cheery mountain brook rushed merrily along. Near its banks, in front of a poor hut, sat an aged man twisting twine. Accosting him, the old man paid no attention; he repeated his salutation, when the old man, surveying him from head to foot, said: "In the government service age does not count for much, there rank is every thing; an aged man may have to bow to a younger, who is his superior officer. 'Tis not so in the country, however; here age alone is respected. Then why am I addressed thus by such a miserable looking stripling?" The young man asked his elder's pardon, and then requested him to answer a question. "I hear," says he, "that the new Magistrate is about to marry the gee sang, Chun Yang Ye; is it true?"

"Don't mention her name," said the old man, angrily. "You are not worthy to speak of her. She is dying in prison, because of her loyal devotion to the brute beast who married and deserted her."

Ye Toh Ryung could hear no more. He hurried from the place, and finding his attendants, announced his intention of going at once into the city, lest the officials should hear of his presence and prepare for him. Entering the city, he went direct to Chun Yang Ye's house. It presented little of the former pleasant appearance. Most of the rich furniture had been sold to buy comforts for the imprisoned girl. The mother, seeing him come, and supposing him to be a beggar, almost shrieked at him to get away. "Are you such a stranger, that you don't know the news? My only child is imprisoned, my husband long since dead, my property almost gone, and you come to me for alms. Begone, and learn the news of the town."

"Look! Don't you know me? I am Ye Toh Ryung, your son-in-law," he said.

"Ye Toh Ryung, and a beggar! Oh, it cannot be. Our only hope is in you, and now you are worse than helpless. My poor girl will die."

"What is the matter with her?" said he, pretending.

The woman related the history of the past months in full, not sparing the man in the least, giving him such a rating as only a woman can. He then asked to be taken to the prison, and she accompanied him with a strange feeling of gratification in her heart that after all she was right, and her daughter's confidence was ill-placed. Arriving at the prison, the mother expressed her feelings by calling to her daughter: "Here is your wonderful husband. You have been so anxious to simply see Ye Toh Ryung before you die; here he is; look at the beggar, and see what your devotion amounts to! Curse him and send him away."

The Ussa called to her, and she recognized the voice. "I surely must be dreaming again," she said, as she tried to arise; but she had the huge neck-encircling board upon her shoulders that marked the latest of her tormentor's acts of oppression, and could not get up. Stung by the pain and the calmness of her lover's voice, she sarcastically asked: "Why have you not come to me? Have you been so busy in official life? Have the rivers been so deep and rapid that you dared not cross them? Did you go so far away that it has required all this time to retrace your steps?" And then, regretting her harsh words, she said: "I cannot tell my rapture. I had expected to have to go to Heaven to meet you, and now you are here. Get them to unbind my feet, and remove this yoke from my neck, that I may come to you."

He came to the little window through which food is passed, and looked upon her. As she saw his face and garb, she moaned: "Oh, what have we done to be so afflicted? You cannot help me now; we must die. Heaven has deserted us."

"Yes," he answered; "granting I am poor, yet should we not be happy in our reunion. I have come as I promised, and we will yet be happy. Do yourself no injury, but trust to me."

She called her mother, who sneeringly inquired of what service she could be, now that the longed-for husband had returned in answer to her prayers. She paid no attention to these cruel words, but told her mother of certain jewels she had concealed in a case in her room. "Sell these," she said, "and buy some food and raiment for my husband; take him home and care for him well. Have him sleep on my couch, and do not reproach him for what he cannot help."

He went with the old woman, but soon left to confer with his attendants, who informed him that the next day was the birthday of the Magistrate, and that great preparations were being made for the celebration that would commence early. A great feast, when wine would flow like water, was to take place in the morning. The gee sang from the whole district were to perform for the assembled guests; bands of music were practising for the occasion, and the whole bade fair to be a great, riotous debauch, which would afford the Ussa just the opportunity the consummation of his plans awaited.

Early the next morning the disguised Ussa presented himself at the yamen gate, where the servants jeered at him, telling him: "This is no beggars' feast," and driving him away. He hung around the street, however, listening to the music inside, and finally he made another attempt, which was more successful than the first, for the servants, thinking him crazy, tried to restrain him, when, in the melée, he made a passage and rushed through the inner gate into the court off the reception hall. The annoyed host, red with wine, ordered him at once ejected and the gate men whipped. His order was promptly obeyed, but Ye did not leave the place. He found a break in the outside wall, through which he climbed, and again presented himself before the feasters. While the Prefect was too blind with rage to be able to speak, the stranger said: "I am a beggar, give me food and drink that I, too, may enjoy myself." The guests laughed at the man's presumption, and thinking him crazy, they urged their host to humor him for their entertainment. To which he finally consented, and, sending him some food and wine, bade him stay in a corner and eat.

To the surprise of all, the fellow seemed still discontented, for he claimed that, as the other guests each had a fair gee sang to sing a wine song while they drank, he should be treated likewise. This amused the guests immensely, and they got the master to send one. The girl went with a poor grace, however, saying: "One would think from the looks of you that your poor throat would open to the wine without a song to oil it," and sang him a song that wished him speedy death instead of long life.

After submitting to their taunts for some time, he said, "I thank you for your food and wine and the graciousness of my reception, in return for which I will amuse you by writing you some verses"; and, taking pencil and paper, he wrote: "The oil that enriches the food of the official is but the life blood of the down-trodden people, whose tears are of no more merit in the eyes of the oppressor than the drippings of a burning candle."

When this was read, a troubled look passed over all; the guests shook their heads and assured their host that it meant ill to him. And each began to make excuses, saying that one and another engagement of importance called them hence. The host laughed and bade them be seated, while he ordered attendants to take the intruder and cast him into prison for his impudence. They came to do so, but the Ussa took out his official seal, giving the preconcerted signal meanwhile, which summoned his ready followers. At sight of the King's seal terror blanched the faces of each of the half-drunken men. The wicked host tried to crawl under the house and escape, but he was at once caught and bound with chains. One of the guests in fleeing through an attic-way caught his topknot of hair in a rat-hole, and stood for some time yelling for mercy, supposing that his captors had him. It was as though an earthquake had shaken the house; all was the wildest confusion.

The Ussa put on decent clothes and gave his orders in a calm manner. He sent the Magistrate to the capital at once, and began to look further into the affairs of the office. Soon, however, he sent a chair for Chun Yang Ye, delegating his own servants, and commanding them not to explain what had happened. She supposed that the Magistrate, full of wine, had sent for her, intending to kill her, and she begged the amused servants to call her Toh Ryung to come and stay with her. They assured her that he could not come, as already he too was at the yamen, and she feared that harm had befallen him on her account.

They removed her shackles and bore her to the yamen, where the Ussa addressed her in a changed voice, commanding her to look up and answer her charges. She refused to look up or speak, feeling that the sooner death came the better. Failing in this way, he then asked her in his own voice to just glance at him. Surprised she looked up, and her dazed eyes saw her lover standing there in his proper guise, and with a delighted cry she tried to run to him, but fainted in the attempt, and was borne in his arms to a room. Just then the old woman, coming along with food, which she had brought as a last service to her daughter, heard the good news from the excited throng outside, and dashing away her dishes and their contents, she tore around for joy, crying: "What a delightful birthday surprise for a cruel magistrate!"

All the people rejoiced with the daughter, but no one seemed to think the old mother deserved such good fortune. The Ussa's conduct was approved at court. A new magistrate was appointed. The marriage was publicly solemnized at Seoul, and the Ussa was raised to a high position, in which he was just to the people, who loved him for his virtues, while the country rang with the praises of his faithful wife, who became the mother of many children.

SIM CHUNG, THE DUTIFUL DAUGHTER.

Sim Hyun, or Mr. Sim, was highly esteemed in the Korean village in which he resided. He belonged to the *Yang Ban*, or gentleman class, and when he walked forth it was with the stately swinging stride of the gentleman, while if he bestrode his favorite donkey, or was carried in his chair, a runner went ahead calling out to the commoners to clear the road. His rank was not high, and though greatly esteemed as a scholar, his income would scarcely allow of his taking the position he was fitted to occupy.

His parents had been very fortunate in betrothing him to a remarkably beautiful and accomplished maiden, daughter of a neighboring gentleman. She was noted for beauty and grace, while her mental qualities were the subject of continual admiration. She could not only read and write her native *ernmun*, but was skilled in Chinese characters, while her embroidered shoes, pockets, and other feminine articles were the pride of her mother and friends. She had embroidered a set of historic panels, which her father sent to the King. His Majesty mentioned her skill with marked commendation, and had the panels made up into a screen which for some time stood behind his mat, and continually called forth his admiration.

Sim had not seemed very demonstrative in regard to his approaching nuptials, but once he laid his eyes upon his betrothed, as she unveiled at the ceremony, he was completely captivated, and brooked with poor grace the formalities that had to be gone through before he could claim her as his constant companion.

It was an exceptionally happy union, the pair being intellectually suited to each other, and each apparently possessing the bodily attributes necessary to charm the other. There was never a sign of disgust or disappointment at the choice their parents had made for them. They used to wander out into the little garden off the women's quarters, and sit in the moonlight, planning for the future, and enjoying the products of each other's well stored mind. It was their pet desire to have a son, and all their plans seemed to centre around this one ambition; the years came and went, however, but their coveted blessing was withheld, the wife consulted priestesses, and the husband, from long and great disappointment, grew sad at heart and cared but little for mingling with the world, which he thought regarded him with shame. He took to books and began to confine himself to his own apartments, letting his poor wife stay neglected and alone in the apartments of the women. From much study, lack of exercise, and failing appetite, he grew thin and emaciated, and his eyes began to show the wear of over-work and innutrition. The effect upon his wife was also bad, but, with a woman's fortitude and patience, she bore up and hoped in spite of constant disappointment. She worried over her husband's condition and felt ashamed that she had no name in the world, other than the wife of Sim, while she wished to be known as the mother of the Sim of whom they had both dreamed by day and by night till dreams had almost left them.

After fifteen years of childless waiting, the wife of Sim dreamed again; this time her vision was a brilliant one, and in it she saw a star come down to her from the skies above; the dream awakened her, and she sent for her husband to tell him that she knew their blessing was about to come to them; she was right, a child was given to them, but, to their great dismay, it was only a girl. Heaven had kindly prepared the way for the little visitor, however; for after fifteen years weary waiting, they were not going to look with serious disfavor upon a girl, however much their hopes had been placed upon the advent of a son.

The child grew, and the parents were united as they only could be by such a precious bond. The ills of childhood seemed not to like the little one, even the virus of small-pox, that was duly placed in her nostril, failed to innoculate her, and her pretty skin remained fresh and soft like velvet, and totally free from the marks of the dread disease.

At three years of age she bade fair to far surpass her mother's noted beauty and accomplishments. Her cheeks were full-blown roses, and whenever she opened her dainty curved mouth, ripples of silvery laughter, or words of mature wisdom, were sure to be given forth. The hearts of the parents, that had previously been full of tears, were now light, and full of contentment and joy; while they were constantly filled with pride by the reports of the wonderful wisdom of their child that continually came to them. The father forgot that his offspring was not a boy, and had his child continually by his side to guide his footsteps, as his feeble eyes refused to perform their office.

Just as their joy seemed too great to be lasting, it was suddenly checked by the death of the mother, which plunged them into a deep grief from which the father emerged totally blind. It soon became a question as to where the daily food was to come from; little by little household trinkets were given to the brokers to dispose of, and in ten years they had used up the homestead, and all it contained.

The father was now compelled to ask alms, and as his daughter was grown to womanhood, she could no longer direct his footsteps as he wandered out in the darkness of the blind.[3] One day in his journeying he fell into a deep ditch, from which he could not extricate himself. After remaining in this deplorable

---

3. After reaching girlhood persons of respectability are not seen on the streets in Korea.

condition for some time he heard a step, and called out for assistance, saying: "I am blind, not drunk," whereupon the passing stranger said: "I know full well you are not drunk. True, you are blind, yet not incurably so."

"Why, who are you that you know so much about me?" asked the blind man.

"I am the old priest of the temple in the mountain fortress."

"Well, what is this that you say about my not being permanently blind?"

"I am a prophet, and I have had a vision concerning you. In case you make an offering of three hundred bags of rice to the Buddha of our temple, you will be restored to sight, you will be given rank and dignity, while your daughter will become the first woman in all Korea."

"But I am poor, as well as blind," was the reply. "How can I promise such a princely offering?"

"You may give me your order for it, and pay it along as you are able," said the priest.

"Very well, give me pencil and paper," whereupon they retired to a house, and the blind man gave his order for the costly price of his sight. Returning home weary, bruised, and hungry, he smiled to himself, in spite of his ill condition, at the thought of his giving an order for so much rice when he had not a grain of it to eat.

He obtained, finally, a little work in pounding rice in the stone mortars. It was hard labor for one who had lived as he had done; but it kept them from starving, and his daughter prepared his food for him as nicely as she knew how. One night, as the dinner was spread on the little, low table before him, sitting on the floor, the priest came and demanded his pay; the old blind man lost his appetite for his dinner, and refused to eat. He had to explain to his daughter the compact he had made with the priest, and, while she was filled with grief, and dismayed at the enormity of the price, she yet seemed to have some hope that it might be accomplished and his sight restored.

That night, after her midnight bath, she lay down on a mat in the open air, and gazed up to heaven, to which she prayed that her poor father might be restored to health and sight. While thus engaged, she fell asleep and dreamed that her mother came down from heaven to comfort her, and told her not to worry, that a means would be found for the payment of the rice, and that soon all would be happy again in the little family.

The next day she chanced to hear of the wants of a great merchant who sailed in his large boats to China for trade, but was greatly distressed by an evil spirit that lived in the water through which he must pass. For some time, it was stated, he had not been able to take his boats over this dangerous place, and his loss therefrom was very great. At last it was reported that he was willing and anxious to appease the spirit by making the offering the wise men had deemed necessary. Priests had told him that the sacrifice of a young maiden to the spirit would quiet it and remove the trouble. He was, therefore, anxious to find the proper person, and had offered a great sum to obtain such an one.

Sim Chung (our heroine), hearing of this, decided that it must be the fulfilment of her dream, and having determined to go and offer herself, she put on old clothes and fasted while journeying, that she might look wan and haggard, like one in mourning. She had previously prepared food for her father, and explained to him that she wished to go and bow at her mother's grave, in return to her for having appeared to her in a dream.

When the merchant saw the applicant, he was at once struck with her beauty and dignity of carriage, in spite of her attempt to disguise herself. He said that it was not in his heart to kill people especially maidens of such worth as she seemed to be. He advised her not to apply; but she told her story and said she would give herself for the three hundred bags of rice. "Ah! now I see the true nobility of your character. I did not know that such filial piety existed outside the works of the ancients. I will send to my master and secure the rice," said the man, who happened to be but an overseer for a greater merchant.

She got the rice and took it to the priest in a long procession of one hundred and fifty ponies, each laboring under two heavy bags; the debt cancelled and her doom fixed, she felt the relaxation and grief necessarily consequent upon such a condition. She could not explain to her father, she mourned over the loneliness that would come to him after she was gone, and wondered how he would support himself after she was removed and until his sight should be restored. She lay down and prayed to heaven, saying: "I am only fourteen years old, and have but four more hours to live. What will become of my poor father? Oh! who will care for him? Kind heaven, protect him when I am gone." Wild with grief she went and sat on her father's knee, but could not control her sobs and tears; whereupon he asked her what the trouble could be. Having made up her mind that the time had come, and that the deed was done and could not be remedied, she decided to tell him, and tried to break it gently; but when the whole truth dawned upon the poor old man it nearly killed him. He clasped her close to his bosom, and crying: "My child, my daughter, my only comfort, I will not let you go. What will eyes be to me if I can no longer look upon your lovely face?" They mingled their tears and sobs, and the neighbors, hearing the commotion in the usually quiet hut, came to see what was the trouble. Upon ascertaining the reason of the old man's grief, they united in the general wailing. Sim Chung begged them to come and care for the old man when she could look after him no more, and they agreed to do so. While the wailing and heart breaking was going on, a stranger rode up on a donkey and asked for the Sim family. He came just in time to see what the act was costing the poor people. He comforted the girl by giving her a cheque for fifty bags of rice for the support of the father when his daughter should be no more. She took it gratefully and gave it to the neighbors to keep in trust; she then prepared herself, took a last farewell, and left her fainting father to go to her bed in the sea.

In due time the boat that bore Sim Chung, at the head of a procession of boats, arrived at the place where the evil spirit reigned. She was dressed in bridal garments furnished by the merchant. On her arrival at the place, the kind merchant tried once more to appease the spirit by an offering of eatables, but it was useless, whereupon Sim Chung prayed to heaven, bade them all good-by, and leaped into the sea. Above, all was quiet, the waves subsided, the sea became like a lake, and the boats passed on their way unmolested.

When Sim Chung regained her consciousness she was seated in a little boat drawn by fishes, and pretty maidens were giving her to drink from a carved jade bottle. She asked them who they were, and where she was going. They answered: "We are servants of the King of the Sea, and we are taking you to his palace."

Sim Chung wondered if this was death, and thought it very pleasant if it were. They passed through forests of waving plants, and saw great lazy fish feeding about in the water, till at last they reached the confines of the palace. Her amazement was then unbounded, for the massive walls were composed of precious stones, such as she had only heretofore seen used as ornaments. Pearls were used to cover the heads of nails in the great doors through which they passed, and everywhere there seemed a most costly and lavish display of the precious gems and metals, while the walks were made of polished black marble that shone in the water. The light, as it passed through the water, seemed to form most beautifully colored clouds, and the rainbow colors were everywhere disporting themselves.

Soon a mighty noise was heard, and they moved aside, while the King passed by preceded by an army with gayly colored and beautifully embroidered satin banners, each bearer blowing on an enormous shell. The King was borne in a golden chair on the shoulders of one hundred men, followed by one hundred musicians and as many more beautiful "dancing girls," with wonderful head-dresses and rich costumes.

Sim Chung objected to going before such an august king, but she was assured of kind treatment, and, after being properly dressed by the sea maids, in garments suitable for the palace of the Sea King, she was borne in a chair on the shoulders of eunuchs to the King's apartments. The King treated her with great respect, and all the maidens and eunuchs bowed before her. She protested that she was not worthy of such attention. "I am," she said, "but the daughter of a beggar, for whom I thought I was giving my life when rescued by these maidens. I am in no way worthy of your respect."

The King smiled a little, and said: "Ah! I know more of you than you know of yourself. You must know that I am the Sea King, and that we know full well the doings of the stars which shine in the heaven above, for they continually visit us on light evenings. Well, you were once a star. Many say a beautiful one, for you had many admirers. You favored one star more than the others, and, in your attentions to him, you abused your office as cup-bearer to the King of Heaven, and let your lover have free access to all of the choice wines of the palace. In this way, before you were aware of it, the peculiar and choice brands that the King especially liked were consumed, and, upon examination, your fault became known. As punishment, the King decided to banish you to earth, but fearing to send you both at once, lest you might be drawn together there, he sent your lover first, and after keeping you in prison for a long time, you were sent as daughter to your former lover. He is the man you claim as father. Heaven has seen your filial piety, however, and repents. You will be hereafter most highly favored, as a reward for your dutiful conduct." He then sent her to fine apartments prepared for her, where she was to rest and recuperate before going back to earth.

After a due period of waiting and feasting on royal food, Sim Chung's beauty was more than restored. She had developed into a complete woman, and her beauty was dazzling; her cheeks seemed colored by the beautiful tints of the waters through which she moved with ease and comfort, while her mind blossomed forth like a flower in the rare society of the Sea King and his peculiarly gifted people.

When the proper time arrived for her departure for the world she had left, a large and beautiful flower was brought into her chamber. It was so arranged that Sim Chung could conceal herself inside of it, while the delicious perfume and the juice of the plant were ample nourishment. When she had bidden good-by to her peculiar friends and taken her place inside the flower, it was conveyed to the surface of the sea, at the place where she had plunged in. She had not waited long in this strange position before a boat bore in sight. It proved to be the vessel of her friend the merchant. As he drew near his old place of danger he marvelled much at sight of such a beautiful plant, growing and blossoming in such a strange place, where once only evil was to be expected. He was also well-nigh intoxicated by the powerful perfume exhaled from the plant. Steering close he managed to secure the flower and place it safely in his boat, congratulating himself on securing so valuable and curious a present for his King. For he decided at once to present it at the palace if he could succeed in getting it safely there.

The plan succeeded, the strange plant with its stranger tenant was duly presented to His Majesty, who was delighted with the gift, and spent his time gazing upon it to the exclusion of state business. He had a glass house prepared for it in an inner court, and seemed never to tire of watching his new treasure.

At night, when all was quiet, Sim Chung was wont to come forth and rest herself by walking in the moonlight. But, on one occasion, the King, being indisposed and restless, thought he would go to breathe the rich perfume of the strange flower and rest himself. In this way he chanced to see Sim Chung before she could conceal herself, and, of course, his surprise was unbounded. He accosted her, not without fear, demanding who she might be. She, being also afraid, took refuge in her flower, when, to the amazement of both, the flower vanished, leaving her standing alone where it had been but a moment before. The King was about to flee, at this point, but

she called to him not to fear, that she was but a human being, and
no spirit as he doubtless supposed. The King drew near, and was at
once lost in admiration of her matchless beauty, when a great noise
was heard outside, and eunuchs came, stating that all the generals
with the heads of departments were asking for an audience on
very important business. His Majesty very reluctantly went to see
what it all meant. An officer versed in astronomy stated that they
had, on the previous night, observed a brilliant star descend from
heaven and alight upon the palace, and that they believed it boded
good to the royal family. Then the King told of the flower, and
the wonderful apparition he had seen in the divine maiden. It so
happened that the queen was deceased, and it was soon decided
that the King should take this remarkable maiden for his wife. The
marriage was announced, and preparations all made. As the lady
was without parents, supposably, the ceremony took place at the
royal wedding hall, and was an occasion of great state.

Never was man more charmed by woman than in this case. The
King would not leave her by day or night, and the business of state
was almost totally neglected. At last Sim Chung chided her husband,
telling him it was not manly for the King to spend all his time in the
women's quarters; that if he cared so little for the rule as to neglect
it altogether, others might find occasion to usurp his place. She
enjoined upon him the necessity of giving the days to his business,
and being content to spend the nights with her. He saw her wisdom,
and remarked upon it, promising to abide by her advice.

After some time spent in such luxury, Sim Chung became lonely
and mourned for her poor father, but despaired of being able to see
him. She knew not if he were alive or dead, and the more she thought
of it the more she mourned, till tears were in her heart continually,
and not infrequently overflowed from her beautiful eyes. The King
chanced to see her weeping, and was solicitous to know the cause
of her sorrow, whereupon she answered that she was oppressed by
a strange dream concerning a poor blind man, and was desirous of
alleviating in some way the sufferings of the many blind men in the

country. Again the King marvelled at her great heart, and offered to do any thing towards carrying out her noble purpose. Together they agreed that they would summon all the blind men of the country to a great feast, at which they should be properly clothed, amply fed, and treated each to a present of cash.

The edict was issued, and on the day appointed for the feast, the Queen secreted herself in a pavilion, from which she could look down and fully observe the strange assemblage. She watched the first day, but saw no one who resembled her lost parent; again the second day she held her earnest vigil, but in vain. She was about to give up her quest as useless and mourn over the loss of her father, when, as the feast was closing on the third day, a feeble old man in rags came tottering up. The attendants, having served so many, were treating this poor fellow with neglect, and were about to drive him away as too late when the Queen ordered them whipped and the old man properly fed.

He seemed well-nigh starved, and grasped at the food set before him with the eagerness of an animal. There seemed to be something about this forlorn creature that arrested and engaged the attention of the Queen, and the attendants, noticing this, were careful to clothe him with extra care. When sufficient time had elapsed for the satisfying of his hunger, he was ordered brought to the Queen's pavilion, where Her Majesty scrutinized him closely for a few moments, and then, to the surprise and dismay of all her attendants, she screamed: "My father! my father!" and fell at his feet senseless. Her maids hurried off to tell the King of the strange conduct of their mistress, and he came to see for himself. By rubbing her limbs and applying strong-smelling medicines to her nostrils, the fainting Queen was restored to consciousness, and allowed to tell her peculiar and interesting story. The King had heard much of it previously. But the poor old blind man could barely collect his senses sufficiently to grasp the situation. As the full truth began to dawn upon him, he cried: "Oh! my child, can the dead come back to us? I hear your voice; I feel your form; but how can I know it is you, for I have no eyes? Away with these sightless orbs!" And he tore at his eyes with his nails, when to his utter amazement and joy, the scales fell away, and he stood rejoicing in his sight once more.

His Majesty was overjoyed to have his lovely Queen restored to her wonted happy frame of mind. He made the old man an officer of high rank, appointed him a fine house, and had him married to the accomplished daughter of an officer of suitable rank, thereby fulfilling the last of the prophecy of both the aged priest and the King of the Sea.

HONG KIL TONG OR, THE ADVENTURES OF AN ABUSED BOY

During the reign of the third king in Korea there lived a noble of high rank and noted family, by name Hong. His title was Ye Cho Pansa. He had two sons by his wife and one by one of his concubines. The latter son was very remarkable from his birth to his death, and he it is who forms the subject of this history.

When Hong Pansa was the father of but two sons, he dreamed by night on one occasion that he heard the noise of thunder, and looking up he saw a huge dragon entering his apartment, which seemed too small to contain the whole of his enormous body. The dream was so startling as to awaken the sleeper, who at once saw that it was a good omen, and a token to him of a blessing about to be conferred. He hoped the blessing might prove to be another son, and went to impart the good news to his wife. She would not see him, however, as she was offended by his taking a concubine from the class of "dancing girls." The great man was sad, and went away. Within the year, however, a son of marvellous beauty was born to one concubine, much to the annoyance of his wife and to himself, for he would have been glad to have the beautiful boy a full son, and eligible to office. The child was named Kil Tong, or Hong Kil Tong. He grew fast, and became more and more beautiful. He learned rapidly, and surprised every one by his remarkable ability. As he grew up he rebelled at being placed with the slaves, and at not being allowed to call his parent, father. The other children laughed and jeered at him, and made life very

miserable. He refused longer to study of the duties of children
to their parents. He upset his table in school, and declared he was
going to be a soldier. One bright moonlight night Hong Pansa
saw his son in the court-yard practising the arts of the soldier,
and he asked him what it meant. Kil Tong answered that he was
fitting himself to become a man that people should respect and
fear. He said he knew that heaven had made all things for the use
of men, if they found themselves capable of using them, and that
the laws of men were only made to assist a few that could not
otherwise do as they would; but that he was not inclined to submit
to any such tyranny, but would become a great man in spite of his
evil surroundings. "This is a most remarkable boy," mused Hong
Pansa. "What a pity that he is not my proper and legitimate son,
that he might be an honor to my name. As it is, I fear he will cause
me serious trouble." He urged the boy to go to bed and sleep, but
Kil Tong said it was useless, that if he went to bed he would think
of his troubles till the tears washed sleep away from his eyes, and
caused him to get up.

The wife of Hong Pansa and his other concubine (the dancing
girl), seeing how much their lord and master thought of Kil Tong,
grew to hate the latter intensely, and began to lay plans for ridding
themselves of him. They called some *mootang*, or sorceresses, and
explained to them that their happiness was disturbed by this son
of a rival, and that peace could only be restored to their hearts
by the death of this youth. The witches laughed and said: "Never
mind. There is an old woman who lives by the east gate, tell her
to come and prejudice the father. She can do it, and he will then
look after his son."

The old hag came as requested. Hong Pansa was then in the
women's apartments, telling them of the wonderful boy, much to
their annoyance. A visitor was announced, and the old woman
made a low bow outside. Hong Pansa asked her what her business
was, and she stated that she had heard of his wonderful son, and

came to see him, to foretell what his future was to be.

Kil Tong came as called, and on seeing him the hag bowed and said: "Send out all of the people." She then stated: "This will be a very great man; if not a king, he will be greater than the king, and will avenge his early wrongs by killing all his family." At this the father called to her to stop, and enjoined strict secrecy upon her. He sent Kil Tong at once to a strong room, and had him locked in for safe keeping.

The boy was very sad at this new state of affairs, but as his father let him have books, he got down to hard study, and learned the Chinese works on astronomy. He could not see his mother, and his unnatural father was too afraid to come near him. He made up his mind, however, that as soon as he could get out he would go to some far off country, where he was not known, and make his true power felt.

Meanwhile, the unnatural father was kept in a state of continual excitement by his wicked concubine, who was bent on the destruction of the son of her rival, and kept constantly before her master the great dangers that would come to him from being the parent of such a man as Kil Tong was destined to be, if allowed to live. She showed him that such power as the boy was destined to possess, would eventually result in his overthrowal, and with him his father's house would be in disgrace, and, doubtless, would be abolished. While if this did not happen, the son was sure to kill his family, so that, in either case, it was the father's clear duty to prevent any further trouble by putting the boy out of the way. Hong Pansa was finally persuaded that his concubine was right, and sent for the assassins to come and kill his son. But a spirit filled the father with disease, and he told the men to stay their work. Medicines failed to cure the disease, and the *mootang* women were called in by the concubine. They beat their drums and danced about the room, conjuring the spirit to leave, but it would not obey. At last they said, at the suggestion of the concubine, that Kil Tong was the cause of the disorder, and that with his death the spirit would cease troubling the father.

Again the assassins were sent for, and came with their swords, accompanied by the old hag from the east gate. While they were meditating on the death of Kil Tong, he was musing on the unjust laws of men who allowed sons to be born of concubines, but denied them rights that were enjoyed by other men.

While thus musing in the darkness of the night, he heard a crow caw three times and fly away. "This means something ill to me," thought he; and just then his window was thrown open, and in stepped the assassins. They made at the boy, but he was not there. In their rage they wounded each other, and killed the old woman who was their guide. To their amazement the room had disappeared, and they were surrounded by high mountains. A mighty storm arose, and rocks flew through the air. They could not escape, and, in their terror, were about to give up, when music was heard, and a boy came riding by on a donkey, playing a flute. He took away their weapons, and showed himself to be Kil Tong. He promised not to kill them, as they begged for their lives, but only on condition that they should never try to kill another man. He told them that he would know if the promise was broken, and, in that event, he would instantly kill them.

Kil Tong went by night to see his father, who thought him a spirit, and was very much afraid. He gave his father medicine, which instantly cured him; and sending for his mother, bade her good-by, and started for an unknown country.

His father was very glad that the boy had escaped, and lost his affection for his wicked concubine. But the latter, with her mistress, was very angry, and tried in vain to devise some means to accomplish their evil purposes.

Kil Tong, free at last, journeyed to the south, and began to ascend the lonely mountains. Tigers were abundant, but he feared them not, and they seemed to avoid molesting him. After many days, he found himself high up on a barren peak enveloped by the clouds, and enjoyed the remoteness of the place, and the absence of men and obnoxious laws. He now felt himself a free man, and the equal of any, while he knew that heaven was smiling upon him and giving him powers not accorded to other men.

Through the clouds at some distance he thought he espied a huge stone door in the bare wall of rock. Going up to it, he found it to be indeed a movable door, and, opening it, he stepped inside, when, to his amazement, he found himself in an open plain, surrounded by high and inaccessible mountains. He saw before him over two hundred good houses, and many men, who, when they had somewhat recovered from their own surprise, came rushing upon him, apparently with evil intent. Laying hold upon him they asked him who he was, and why he came trespassing upon their ground. He said: "I am surprised to find myself in the presence of men. I am but the son of a concubine, and men, with their laws, are obnoxious to me. Therefore, I thought to get away from man entirely, and, for that reason, I wandered alone into these wild regions. But who are you, and why do you live in this lone spot? Perhaps we may have a kindred feeling."

"We are called thieves," was answered; "but we only despoil the hated official class of some of their ill-gotten gains. We are willing to help the poor unbeknown, but no man can enter our stronghold and depart alive, unless he has become one of us. To do so, however, he must prove himself to be strong in body and mind. If you can pass the examination and wish to join our party, well and good; otherwise you die."

This suited Kil Tong immensely, and he consented to the conditions. They gave him various trials of strength, but he chose his own. Going up to a huge rock on which several men were seated, he laid hold of it and hurled it to some distance, to the dismay of the men, who fell from their seat, and to the surprised delight of all. He was at once installed a member, and a feast was ordered. The contract was sealed by mingling blood from the lips of all the members with blood similarly supplied by Kil Tong. He was then given a prominent seat and served to wine and food.

Kil Tong soon became desirous of giving to his comrades some manifestation of his courage. An opportunity presently offered. He heard the men bemoaning their inability to despoil a large and strong Buddhist temple not far distant. As was the rule, this temple in the mountains was well patronized by officials, who made it a place of retirement for pleasure and debauch, and in return the lazy, licentious priests were allowed to collect tribute from the poor people about, till they had become rich and powerful. The several attempts made by the robber band had proved unsuccessful, by virtue of the number and vigilance of the priests, together with the strength of their enclosure. Kil Tong agreed to assist them to accomplish their design or perish in the attempt, and such was their faith in him that they readily agreed to his plans.

On a given day Kil Tong, dressed in the red gown of a youth, just betrothed, covered himself with the dust of travel, and mounted on a donkey, with one robber disguised as a servant, made his way to the temple. He asked on arrival to be shown to the head priest, to whom he stated that he was the son of Hong Pansa, that his noble father having heard of the greatness of this temple, and the wisdom of its many priests, had decided to send him with a letter, which he produced, to be educated among their numbers. He also stated that a train of one hundred ponies loaded with rice had been sent as a present from his father to the priest, and he expected they would arrive before dark, as they did not wish to stop alone in the mountains, even though every pony was attended by a groom, who was armed for defense. The priests were delighted, and having read the letter, they never for a moment suspected that all was not right. A great feast was ordered in honor of their noble scholar, and all sat down before the tables, which were filled so high that one could hardly see his neighbor on the opposite side. They had scarcely seated themselves and indulged in the generous wine, when it was announced that the train of ponies laden with rice had arrived. Servants were sent to look after the tribute, and the eating and drinking went on. Suddenly Kil Tong clapped his hand, over his cheek with a cry of pain, which drew the attention of all. When, to the great mortification of the priests, he produced from his mouth a pebble, previously introduced on the sly, and exclaimed: "Is it to feed on stones that my father sent me to this place? What do you mean by setting such rice before a gentleman?"

The priests were filled with mortification and dismay, and bowed their shaven heads to the floor in humiliation. When at a sign from Kil Tong, a portion of the robbers, who had entered the court as grooms to the ponies, seized the bending priests and bound them as they were. The latter shouted for help, but the other robbers, who had been concealed in the bags, which were supposed to contain rice, seized the servants, while others were loading the ponies with jewels, rice, cash and whatever of value they could lay hands upon.

An old priest who was attending to the fires, seeing the uproar, made off quietly to the yamen near by and called for soldiers. The soldiers were sent after some delay, and Kil Tong, disguised as a priest, called to them to follow him down a by-path after the robbers. While he conveyed the soldiers over this rough path, the robbers made good their escape by the main road, and were soon joined in their stronghold by their youthful leader, who had left the soldiers groping helplessly in the dark among the rocks and trees in a direction opposite that taken by the robbers.

The priests soon found out that they had lost almost all their riches, and were at no loss in determining how the skilful affair had been planned and carried out. Kil Tong's name was noised abroad, and it was soon known that he was heading a band of robbers, who, through his assistance, were able to do many marvellous things. The robber band were delighted at the success of his first undertaking, and made him their chief, with the consent of all. After sufficient time had elapsed for the full enjoyment of their last and greatest success, Kil Tong planned a new raid.

The Governor of a neighboring province was noted for his overbearing ways and the heavy burdens that he laid upon his subjects. He was very rich, but universally hated, and Kil Tong decided to avenge the people and humiliate the Governor, knowing that his work would be appreciated by the people, as were indeed his acts at the temple. He instructed his band to proceed singly to the Governor's city—the local capital—at the time of a fair, when their coming would not cause comment. At a given time a portion of them were to set fire to a lot of straw-thatched huts outside the city gates, while the others repaired in a body to the Governor's yamen. They did so. The Governor was borne in his chair to a place where he could witness the conflagration, which also drew away the most of the inhabitants. The robbers bound the remaining servants, and while some were securing money, jewels, and weapons, Kil Tong wrote on the walls: "The wicked Governor that robs the people is relieved of his ill-gotten gains by Kil Tong—the people's avenger."

Again the thieves made good their escape, and Kil Tong's name became known everywhere. The Governor offered a great reward for his capture, but no one seemed desirous of encountering a robber of such boldness. At last the King offered a reward after consulting with his officers. When one of them said he would capture the thief alone, the King was astonished at his boldness and courage, and bade him be off and make the attempt. The officer was called the Pochang; he had charge of the prisons, and was a man of great courage.

The Pochang started on his search, disguised as a traveller. He took a donkey and servant, and after travelling many days he put up at a little inn, at the same time that another man on a donkey rode up. The latter was Kil Tong in disguise, and he soon entered into conversation with the man, whose mission was known to him.

"*I goo*," said Kil Tong, as he sat down to eat, "this is a dangerous country. I have just been chased by the robber Kil Tong till the life is about gone out of me."

"Kil Tong, did you say?" remarked Pochang. "I wish he would chase me. I am anxious to see the man of whom we hear so much."

"Well, if you see him once you will be satisfied," replied Kil Tong.

"Why?" asked the Pochang. "Is he such a fearful-looking man as to frighten one by his aspect alone?"

"No; on the contrary he looks much as do ordinary mortals. But we *know* he is different, you see."

"Exactly," said the Pochang. "That is just the trouble. You are afraid of him before you see him. Just let me get a glimpse of him, and matters will be different, I think."

"Well," said Kil Tong, "you can be easily pleased, if that is all, for I dare say if you go back into the mountains here you will see him, and get acquainted with him too."

"That is good. Will you show me the place?"

"Not I. I have seen enough of him to please me. I can tell you where to go, however, if you persist in your curiosity," said the robber.

"Agreed!" exclaimed the officer. "Let us be off at once lest he escapes. And if you succeed in showing him to me, I will reward you for your work and protect you from the thief."

After some objection by Kil Tong, who appeared to be reluctant to go, and insisted on at least finishing his dinner, they started off, with their servants, into the mountains. Night overtook them, much to the apparent dismay of the guide, who pretended to be very anxious to give up the quest. At length, however, they came to the stone door, which was open. Having entered the robber's stronghold, the door closed behind them, and the guide disappeared, leaving the dismayed officer surrounded by the thieves. His courage had now left him, and he regretted his rashness. The robbers bound him securely and led him past their miniature city into an enclosure surrounded by houses which, by their bright colors, seemed to be the abode of royalty. He was conveyed into a large audience-chamber occupying the most extensive building of the collection, and there, on a sort of throne, in royal style, sat his guide. The Pochang saw his mistake, and fell on his face, begging for mercy. Kil Tong upbraided him for his impudence and arrogance and promised to let him off this time. Wine was brought, and all partook of it. That given to the officer was drugged, and he fell into a stupor soon after drinking it. While in this condition he was put into a bag and conveyed in a marvellous manner to a high mountain overlooking the capital. Here he found himself upon recovering from the effects of his potion; and not daring to face his sovereign with such a fabulous tale, he cast himself down from the high mountain, and was picked up dead, by passers-by, in the morning. Almost at the same time that His Majesty received word of the death of his officer, and was marvelling at the audacity of the murderer in bringing the body almost to the palace doors, came simultaneous reports of great depredations in each of the eight provinces. The trouble was in each case attributed to Kil Tong, and the fact that he was reported as being in eight far removed places at the same time caused great consternation.

Official orders were issued to each of the eight governors to catch and bring to the city, at once, the robber Kil Tong. These orders were so well obeyed that upon a certain day soon after, a guard came from each province bringing Kil Tong, and there in a line stood eight men alike in every respect.

The King on inquiry found that Kil Tong was the son of Hong Pansa, and the father was ordered into the royal presence. He came with his legitimate son, and bowed his head in shame to the ground.

When asked what he meant by having a son who would cause such general misery and distress, he swooned away, and would have died had not one of the Kil Tongs produced some medicine which cured him. The son, however, acted as spokesman, and informed the King that Kil Tong was but the son of his father's slave, that he was utterly incorrigible, and had fled from home when a mere boy. When asked to decide as to which was his true son, the father stated that his son had a scar on the left thigh. Instantly each of the eight men pulled up the baggy trousers and displayed a scar. The guard was commanded to remove the men and kill all of them; but when they attempted to do so the life had disappeared, and the men were found to be only figures in straw and wax.

Soon after this a letter was seen posted on the Palace gate, announcing that if the government would confer upon Kil Tong the rank of Pansa, as held by his father, and thus remove from him the stigma attaching to him as the son of a slave, he would stop his depredations. This proposition could not be entertained at first, but one of the counsel suggested that it might offer a solution of the vexed question, and they could yet be spared the disgrace of having an officer with such a record. For, as he proposed, men could be so stationed that when the newly-appointed officer came to make his bow before His Majesty, they could fall upon him and kill him before he arose. This plan was greeted with applause, and a decree was issued conferring the desired rank; proclamations to that effect being posted in public places, so that the news would reach Kil Tong. It did reach him, and he soon appeared at the city gate. A great crowd attended him as he rode to the Palace gates; but knowing the plans laid for him, as he passed through the gates and came near enough to be seen of the King, he was caught up in a cloud and borne away amid strange music; wholly discomfiting his enemies.

Some time after this occurrence the King was walking with a few eunuchs and attendants in the royal gardens. It was evening time, but the full moon furnished ample light. The atmosphere was tempered just to suit; it was neither cold nor warm, while it lacked nothing of the bracing character of a Korean autumn. The leaves were blood-red on the maples; the heavy cloak of climbing vines that enshrouded the great wall near by was also beautifully colored. These effects could even be seen by the bright moonlight, and seated on a hill-side the royal party were enjoying the tranquillity of the scene, when all were astonished by the sound of a flute played by some one up above them. Looking up among the tree-tops a man was seen descending toward them, seated upon the back of a gracefully moving stork. The King imagined it must be some heavenly being, and ordered the chief eunuch to make some proper salutation. But before this could be done, a voice was heard saying: "Fear not, O King. I am simply Hong Pansa [Kil Tong's new title]. I have come to make my obeisance before your august presence and be confirmed in my rank."

This he did, and no one attempted to molest him; seeing which, the King, feeling that it was useless longer to attempt to destroy a man who could read the unspoken thoughts of men, said:

"Why do you persist in troubling the country? I have removed from you now the stigma attached to your birth. What more will you have?"

"I wish," said Kil Tong, with due humility, "to go to a distant land, and settle down to the pursuit of peace and happiness. If I may be granted three thousand bags of rice I will gladly go and trouble you no longer."

"But how will you transport such an enormous quantity of rice?" asked the King.

"That can be arranged," said Kil Tong. "If I may be but granted the order, I will remove the rice at daybreak."

The order was given. Kil Tong went away as he came, and in the early morning a fleet of junks appeared off the royal granaries, took on the rice, and made away before the people were well aware of their presence.

Kil Tong now sailed for an island off the west coast. He found one uninhabited, and with his few followers he stored his riches, and brought many articles of value from his former hiding-places. His people he taught to till the soil, and all went well on the little island till the master made a trip to a neighboring island, which was famous for its deadly mineral poison,—a thing much prized for tipping the arrows with. Kil Tong wanted to get some of this poison, and made a visit to the island. While passing through the settled districts he casually noticed that many copies of a proclamation were posted up, offering a large reward to any one who would succeed in restoring to her father a young lady who had been stolen by a band of savage people who lived in the mountains.

Kil Tong journeyed on all day, and at night he found himself high up in the wild mountain regions, where the poison was abundant. Gazing about in making some preparations for passing the night in this place, he saw a light, and following it, he came to a house built below him on a ledge of rocks, and in an almost inaccessible position. He could see the interior of a large hall, where were gathered many hairy, shaggy-looking men, eating, drinking, and smoking. One old fellow, who seemed to be chief, was tormenting a young lady by trying to tear away her veil and expose her to the gaze of the barbarians assembled. Kil Tong could not stand this sight, and, taking a poisoned arrow, he sent it direct for the heart of the villain, but the distance was so great that he missed his mark sufficiently to only wound the arm. All were amazed, and in the confusion the girl escaped, and Kil Tong concealed himself for the night. He was seen next day by some of the savage band, who caught him, and demanded who he was and why he was found in the mountains. He answered that he was a physician, and had come up there to collect a certain rare medicine only known to exist in those mountains.

The robbers seemed rejoiced, and explained that their chief had been wounded by an arrow from the clouds, and asked him if he could cure him. Kil Tong was taken in and allowed to examine the chief, when he agreed to cure him within three days. Hastily mixing up some of the fresh poison, he put it into the wound, and the chief died almost at once. Great was the uproar when the death became known. All rushed at the doctor, and would have killed him, but Kil Tong, finding his own powers inadequate, summoned to his aid his old friends the spirits (*quay sin*), and swords flashed in the air, striking off heads at every blow, and not ceasing till the whole band lay weltering in their own blood.

Bursting open a door, Kil Tong saw two women sitting with covered faces, and supposing them to be of the same strange people, he was about to dispatch them on the spot, when one of them threw aside her veil and implored for mercy. Then it was that Kil Tong recognized the maiden whom he had rescued the previous evening. She was marvellously beautiful, and already he was deeply smitten with her maidenly charms. Her voice seemed like that of an angel of peace sent to quiet the hearts of rough men. As she modestly begged for her life, she told the story of her capture by the robbers, and how she had been dragged away to their den, and was only saved from insult by the interposition of some heavenly being, who had in pity smote the arm of her tormentor.

Great was Kil Tong's joy at being able to explain his own part in the matter, and the maiden heart, already won by the manly beauty of her rescuer, now overflowed with gratitude and love. Remembering herself, however, she quickly veiled her face, but the mischief had been done; each had seen the other, and they could henceforth know no peace, except in each other's presence.

The proclamations had made but little impression upon Kil Tong, and it was not till the lady had told her story that he remembered reading them. He at once took steps to remove the beautiful girl and her companion in distress, and not knowing but that other of the savages might return, he did not dare to make search for a chair and bearers, but mounting donkeys the little party set out for the home of the distressed parents, which they reached safely in due time. The father's delight knew no bounds. He was a subject of Korea's King, yet he possessed this island and ruled its people in his own right. And calling his subjects, he explained to them publicly the wonderful works of the stranger, to whom he betrothed his daughter, and to whom he gave his official position.

The people indulged in all manner of gay festivities in honor of the return of the lost daughter of their chief; in respect to the bravery of Kil Tong; and to celebrate his advent as their ruler.

In due season the marriage ceremonies were celebrated, and the impatient lovers were given to each other's embrace. Their lives were full of happiness and prosperity. Other outlying islands were united under Kil Tong's rule, and no desire or ambition remained ungratified. Yet there came a time when the husband grew sad, and tears swelled the heart of the young wife as she tried in vain to comfort him. He explained at last that he had a presentiment that his father was either dead or dying, and that it was his duty to go and mourn at the grave. With anguish at the thought of parting, the wife urged him to go. Taking a junk laden with handsome marble slabs for the grave and statuary to surround it, and followed by junks bearing three thousand bags of rice, he set out for the capital. Arriving, he cut off his hair, and repaired to his old home, where a servant admitted him on the supposition that he was a priest. He found his father was no more; but the body yet remained, because a suitable place could not be found for the burial. Thinking him to be a priest, Kil Tong was allowed to select the spot, and the burial took place with due ceremony. Then it was that the son revealed himself, and took his place with the mourners. The stone images and monuments were erected upon the nicely sodded grounds. Kil Tong sent the rice he had brought, to the government granaries

in return for the King's loan to him, and regretted that mourning
would prevent his paying his respects to his King; he set out for
his home with his true mother and his father's legal wife. The latter
did not survive long after the death of her husband, but the poor
slave-mother of the bright boy was spared many years to enjoy the
peace and quiet of her son's bright home, and to be ministered to
by her dutiful, loving children and their numerous offspring.

THE END